B U L L E T T I M E

NICK MAMATAS

ChiZine Publications

FIRST EDITION

Distributed in Canada by
HarperCollins Canada Ltd.
1995 Markham Road
Scarborough, ON M1B 5M8
Toll Free: 1-800-387-0117
e-mail: hcorder@harpercollins.com

Distributed in the U.S. by
Diamond Book Distributors
1966 Greenspring Drive
Timonium, MD 21093
Phone: 1-410-560-7100 x826
e-mail: books@diamondbookdistributors.com

Library and Archives Canada Cataloguing in Publication

Mamatas, Nick
      Bullettime / Nick Mamatas.

Issued also in electronic formats.
ISBN 978-1-926851-71-6

    I. Title.

PS3613.A3539B84 2012   813'.6   C2012-902962-9

CHIZINE PUBLICATIONS
Toronto, Canada
www.chizinepub.com
info@chizinepub.com

Edited and copyedited by Brett Savory
Proofread by Stephen Michell

 Canada Council   Conseil des Arts
for the Arts   du Canada

We acknowledge the support of the Canada Council for the Arts which last year
invested $20.1 million in writing and publishing throughout Canada.

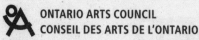
ONTARIO ARTS COUNCIL
CONSEIL DES ARTS DE L'ONTARIO

Published with the generous assistance of the Ontario Arts Council.

Printed in Canada

To nobody.

You know who you are.

BULLETTIME

CHAPTER 1

This is not a story about how to do what I did and survive, and be free. I'm not free. In many of the millions of futures that tumbled forth, that are still rolling and twisting ahead out to the ends of the world since that day, I'm not even alive. She is though, at the end of every strand of fate, tugging on the fabric of life and laughing.

I just happen to think she's laughing with me, not at me. I hope so. I love her. This is the story of my love for her. It's a story that I like to tell from the bottom of a little plastic cup.

O

Tussin. If they only wanted you to take two tablespoons, why would a bottle of the stuff come with a plastic cup that can hold eight? Half a bottle before school, but David Holbrook still uses the little cup instead of just taking a swig out of the bottle. One, *ugh*, two, *blech*, three. Okay, then a fourth. Then a big handful of Coricidin HBP. It wouldn't look like Skittles if they weren't supposed to be eaten by the handful. *To the mirror, Mr. Holbrook*, he thinks. David liked thinking of himself as Mr. Holbrook. He wished he attended an uptight boarding school like on TV, where the teachers called the students Mr. Thomason and Mr. Smythe and the older boys who tortured the freshmen with wristlocks and spittle and the Greek alphabet gave everyone clever nicknames: Foggy, Banger, Lilliput.

David's actual nickname at school is "Hey Fag." When he thinks of himself in casual terms, he's Dave.

Five. *Yuck*. Six. Water, water. Seven. *Gah*. Grape-mediciny. Robotrippin'.

To the mirror, Mr. Holbrook.

Dave looks into the mirror. He can't take himself all in at once, not with the drugs still gurgling in his stomach, and not yet completely bathing his brain, but he can look. Two eyes, brown. Red creases like a brand, where his eyeglasses rest on his nose. Hair, too much of it, piled on his head—not long like a dirtbag kid—just thick and wide and untamable. A shoulder, fertile with acne. The crease of a collarbone, hard like the end of a sentence. Streaks of ribs under skin where his pecs should be. That's enough for now.

Dave flows down the steps, past the empty living room and into the kitchen. His mother sits at the table, somewhat preoccupied by the buzz and flicker of the little black and white TV. "Dave," she says, "Dave. Good morning."

"Hi, Ma."

She sighs chemically. "Do you want breakfast? I can make you some," to the TV—the weather will be fine, the traffic is fine—"breakfast. You don't want any breakfast?" Dave's stomach gurgles, all grape and trouble. "It's okay."

8

"Yeah, it's okay." She rises and tries a half smile. "I'm a little tired, out of sorts, you know. I think I'll get some rest. I'll cook you breakfast later." She shuffles past Dave; the few silvery hairs amidst the L'Oréal Cherry Cordial catch the light, and he stares. Mom turns back to him and offers a languid half smile. "Have fun," she says, "at school. Be good. Be careful. Okay? Okay."

Out the door and onto the street. The sun is like butter, smeared everywhere. Dave shakes off the heat from his stomach and the back of his neck, sniffs a bit of tingly grape in his sinuses, and . . . *to school, Mr. Holbrook.* He turns at the end of the block, a right, then a left, then three blocks and a left, onto Pavonia Avenue, where the houses fall away and dusty storefronts yawn, selling faded crap from twenty years before. Sewing machines, American flags faded to pink and baby blue, Coca-Cola cans celebrating June's big movie—it's September. Dave is, I was, fifteen, and there was music in the air. Phat beats from passing cars, the bass so heavy that thumps turned to fuzz. Salsa and the haunting wail of Indian music too; the little restaurants on the street—all of them with signs reading No High School Students Before Lunch Thank You (with various creative misspellings and random apostrophes added)—liked to compete with tinny PA systems.

I see him now, walking down the slope of Pavonia Avenue toward the grey slab of high school, his shoulders sinking, his smile wilting. The music is swallowed by the bellows and shrieks of the kids outside. Like the restaurants, they compete on ethnic grounds: clumps of black kids have the curb, the Latinos have taken the steps, a small brace of whites mill about across the street, waiting till the last possible moment before crossing the street to Palisade Avenue and Hamilton High School. Dave isn't sure if his feet feel heavy and oh so long, as if he's wearing invisible clown shoes, due to his morning ritual, or just because school is nothing but a horrible prison. Devil's Island. Island not included.

As the drugs finally push their way up to Dave's brain, he remembers that he actually likes the school. Not the school as an *encounter*, but as a building. It's a huge Neoclassical Revival building, consuming the whole block, and Palisade meets Newark Avenue on a hill . . . a friggin' hill like out in the country. It smells like another century. Gods and goddesses stand in stony relief over the entranceway. KNOWLEDGE is carved into the upper part of the seal over the entrance. INDUSTRY takes up the lower part. Dave thinks he might be the only kid of the 2,700 in school to have actually read the wall as he waits in line to pass through the metal detectors, and he hasn't looked up since the first day of freshman year.

"Hey, fag!" someone shouts, but since everyone's a fag, a stupid bitch, a niggah, a *maricon*, or an asshole, Dave doesn't look up. Whoever it is was probably talking to someone else. That's what he tells himself.

To school, Mr. Holbrook. That was me, whispering from the Ylem, but he hears it. I think he does. Today is the day. Dave oozes up the steps, his legs leaden, but he's still the first white kid in school. The others are too afraid of the blacks and Latinos to walk the gauntlet, but Dave figured out long ago that nobody gives two shits about him. He's a minnow in the sea. The stone walls of the school waver like he's experiencing a heat fever, even in the cool September air. The half-angry yawps of a thousand taunts and conversations blend into a grinding buzz. Dave walks into school, into the great yawning antechamber that connects the arterial halls, and he looks up.

He is alone, on a plane of existence all his own. Only through the ethereal haze does he see other students—mostly Asian kids with books hugged to their chests, or girls frowning into their pagers, but they are nearly still. Dave thinks of old European churches that he has never seen; he believes the schoolteacher lie about glass being nothing but a very viscous liquid, and how in those cathedrals stained glass bulges and pools in reds and blues ever so slightly over stone sills. The kids are all trapped in glass now, pushing their way through their eternities so slowly that even Dave can barely sense it. He walks past them like he was strolling through a statuary garden, finds homeroom, and slides into his usual desk two rows from the back, to relax for a century or two, until the bell rings and breaks the spell.

There is a noise from the hall, and it isn't the endless baritone of the bells, but a sound like the sun breaking winter on a frozen river. A crushing high-pitched squeal-screech of song: ice against ice. Then she walks in, *she walks in at his speed*, all snaking black curls and almond eyes, the ether collapsing around her like she's walking through plate glass. In a long black coat. An apple in her left hand, Golden Delicious. She takes an enthusiastic bite, smacks her lips and speaks.

Speaks to me!

"Hey, fag," she says, nodding toward the silhouette shimmering in the front of the room by the slate chemistry lab table, "is this Mr. Ottatti's homeroom?"

It wasn't.

Dave opens his mouth to say something, but just comes to with a mouthful of blood. He keels right over and hits the back of his head on the floor. Unconsciousness is full of stars.

CHAPTER 2

I never learned much about classical music, but that day I felt the holy sweep of violins cradling and rocking me like a babe in arms. The flute (was it a flute, or some other, rarer instrument?) whispered the sweetest hints of dreams.

Dave comes to near the big radiator in the nurse's office, which was always and inexplicably whining away to keep the room at a constant temperature of 85 degrees. Dave is clammy, but he was the only one not sweating. Nurse Alvarez, a thick older woman, hovers over him. Her lips are wet with perspiration. Standing over her shoulder is Officer Levine, the friendliest-looking of Hamilton's cops. He's a black guy with a Jewish name, the perfect person to meet parents after a fight or someone's purse goes missing—white parents hear the name and relax a bit before he walks in; black parents like seeing a face of authority that looks a bit like their own. Dave wonders if the school planned it that way, then he wonders why he's even thinking about stuff like this.

"How long was I out?"

"Out? You weren't out," Nurse Alvarez says, "you just walked in here and laid down."

Dave reaches up to his mouth and touches the blood on his lip.

"You bit the inside of your cheek, but it's nothing that needs stitches."

"Are you on drugs?" asks Officer Levine, but he does it in a friendly, joking way, like a television uncle who wants to buy some pot.

"He's not on drugs! Look at him."

"I *am* looking at him, Nurse Alvarez," Levine says. Again: "Are you on drugs, son?" but now his tone is serious, as if he knows the answer.

"He's not on drugs. He's a good kid." Alvarez nods to herself. "I can tell."

"I do . . ." Dave starts. The adults lean in and leer.

"—take allergy medication. I mean, sometimes it might make me dizzy."

Officer Levine glances away to write a note in his little pad, but Nurse Alvarez stares on owlishly. "Allergy medication," she repeats.

"I thought he was a good kid, nurse."

"He *looks* like a good kid."

"Uh . . . I don't think I remember walking here. Do I have a hall pass?"

"Why do you say that? Because he's white?"

"Maybe I should go home, and change my shirt?"

"It could be a health hazard, walking around with all that blood, right, nurse?"

"Oh no, there's no damn health hazard. That's crazy

talk. This school is full of crazy talk."

"How do you know?"

"How would *you* know?"

"Okay, can you give me a hall pass so I can get to first period? I mean, if I'm not under arrest or anything?"

"No, because he's a nerd."

"There's a lot of blood. Is that normal?"

"Oh, it's normal when you're bleeding."

"I've seen men who have been shot who have bled less, actually."

"Yeah, but were they shot on the inside of the cheek? Were they sitting around, drooling all over themselves and humming?"

"Uh, are you two still talking about me?"

"Easy, there, guy. I know this has to be rough for you—"

"Everything's rough for kids like him."

"Like me?"

"Nerds!" hisses the nurse.

Officer Levine laughs a sharp *Ha*! at that. Dave contemplates objecting to the appellation but decides he'd rather spend the rest of the day in a slightly less smelly room. The adults, or at least their stained clothing, both reek. And it's hot, and the radiator is too loud.

Levine tears a page out of his note pad. "Here's your pass. Go right to where you need to go."

Dave isn't quite sure where that is, Social Studies never being all that high on anyone's list of the mandatory, but he takes the note and steps to the door.

"You come back," Nurse Alvarez calls out after him, "if you get any more blood on you."

Dave is glad to walk the near-empty halls, to avoid the hooting, the casually thrust shoulders to his chest, the occasional catcall.

A few kids, cutting or on their way to some errand, mill by a water fountain. They're big kids, seniors—one of them has a friggin' mustache and maybe a few grey hairs in his tight curls—but they don't jeer or call out to him. Instead, they just shut up and look. Dave is nearly upon them when one of them speaks.

"Damn, what happened?" He stares pointedly at Dave's shirt, a powder blue button-down number. Dave thought it was sticking to his chest from the cold sweats, or his time baking by the radiator. Blood, thick and almost purple, coats it like bad tomato sauce.

"You get stabbed or something?" asks another kid. His name's Lee. Dave knows him a bit. Not too bright.

"Naw, it's his lip," says the third guy, the one with the mustache. "Get fucked up? Fall down?"

Dave shrugs. "Something like that."

Lee smiles. "Want us to fuck him up for you? We'll fuck him up good. Got a hundred, we'll kill him. We'll throw his body in the fucking swamp under the overpass. Hundred bucks, just name the motherfucker." He raises his hand, looking for a high-five for something, from his friends if not from Dave. He gets a trio of eyerolls instead.

"Shut the fuck up, Lee," says the mustachioed guy.

"You're gonna go to class like that?" the first kid asks Dave.

"Sure."

"Aww—this we gotta see."

So they march behind him, whatever their previous plans were forgotten. Dave wonders if he should offer a handshake or an introduction, but the mustache does it instead. "I'm Malik. That's Lee—"

"I know this kid!" says Lee. "He's in PE with me. Can't even serve a volleyball. His name's Damien or some shit."

"—and George."

"Yo," says George. "Your name is really Damien? That's the devil's name!"

"Dave," says Dave.

"Naw, it's Damien. I know this kid!"

"Motherfucker, he knows his own fucking name!" says Malik.

Down the steps. Dave lightly, the guys behind him waterfalls of stomping. Then to Room 216 and Social Studies. Dave opens the door and interrupts the lesson. Mr. McCann isn't sure what to say at first. He pushes his glasses up to the bridge of his nose and says, "I hope you have a pass from the nurse, if not the hospital."

Dave steps into the room and the students get their first look. "Well, find a seat, son," McCann says pointedly and just loud enough to cover some of the mumbling of *night of the living dead, yo* and *hope that motherfucker doesn't have AIDS* from the crowd. Dave shuffles to the back by the heavy grated windows, where there are two free desks so he won't have to sit next to anyone. In the doorway, the three older kids stare.

"Can I help you gentlemen?" Mr. McCann asks. "Are you the honour guard or from the CDC?"

"Nah, we're good," says Malik. He doesn't move from the doorway though.

Mr. McCann steps to the door and grips the knob. "Well, so are we. I'm sure you boys have some place to be," he says, and shuts the door.

He walks back to the blackboard in front of the crowded classroom and sighs as he retrieves his chalk from the ledge. A knock on the door. Mr. McCann ignores it and raises his arm. The knock, louder. He answers the door. It's Malik.

"Don't call us *boys*, man," he says. "Damn, don't you know nothing?"

"Malcolm X!" shouts Lee from somewhere out in the hallway.

McCann holds his hands over his heart and says, "You have my deepest apologies. I meant nothing by it. I'm sure you fine, upstanding young men have some place to be." He nudges the door shut with his foot and heads back to the blackboard.

A knock at the door.

McCann ignores it.

A knock at the door. Louder, more insistent.

McCann turns back to the door and opens it.

There she is. She offers McCann a pass. "I'm supposed to be here," she says. "Honours Social, right?"

McCann glances over at the rest of the room. "Such that it is, you are right indeed. Take a seat, Ms.—"

She winds through the rows, passing the few empty seats on the way to the one next to Dave, then she sits and shrugs off her coat, shakes out her hair, and says, "Zevgolis."

McCann turns back to the board, and she turns to Dave.

"Can I offer you a Wetnap, or will you just pass out

again?" She has the little towelette, its foil package decorated with a tiny Acropolis in blue and white, in her hand. Dave stares at it, fighting his drug-brain's anxious desire to transform it into a wrapped condom.

"I think I'm good," he says. Then he spends the rest of the class inhaling deeply. Her hair smells like a symphony.

O

Dave doesn't see the girl in Spanish (*she's sophisticated, probably taking French instead*, I thought at the time), or in his Honours Biology section. Then it was study hall, so Dave decides to look around for her, but Hamilton's hallways weren't cooperating like they normally do. They seem longer, somehow, and hotter. From the Ylem, it was almost embarrassing to watch me back then, a droopy-eyed duck looking for mama. And she is everywhere, if only for a moment. A swath of long, dark hair (whoops, a dude), the swivel of a hip (wrong girl), a bobbing head at about her height (nope, an Asian girl), the shadow of a long coat around the corner (that annoying guy who wore a duster and a fedora every day). And just as everywhere, the gawking and staring as Dave shuffles, smiles, and talks to himself, his shirt coated in drying brown blood. It is enough to make the kids forget his nickname, if just for one day.

"D'ya know where she is?" Dave asks with a squint. He can just barely see me, moving along with him a femtosecond out of sync. Of course I didn't, not at the time. Of course, I didn't have the means to say anything to him either. I can tell you where she was though.

Where she was just then—and her name is Eris and

she is the goddess of discord—was in the main office, leaning over the high desk and spelling her last name for the secretary who was trying vainly to call up her permanent record, a record that was being stitched together, electron by electron, by the goddess herself as she slowly spelled out Z-E-V-G-O-L-I-S. Though it happened outside of my realm of experience, I know this because when she exiled me to the Ylem, she made sure this was the one moment I could see without David Holbrook's eyes.

"Oh, here you are," the secretary said. "Erin."

And Eris yawned and stretched out her arms and set a cup of pencils tumbling onto the keyboard, deleting the N, inputting an S, and pressing the RETURN key all at once, formalizing the record. "Whoops!" she said, like a human might, as the secretary scrambled to pick up the rolling pencils and shove them back into the can.

"Sorry about that," said Eris back then—the first and last time she ever even pretended to apologize for anything.

The secretary just frowned and turned back to her computer and changed Eris's schedule to make sure that all of her classes matched Dave's.

O

"Where is she; is it time for class?" Dave asks himself a little too loudly, like he's alone in the hallway when he's actually not. "I dunno," he answers himself, which is even more dangerous. And here one of them comes, with a meaty palm to the shoulder and a twisted smear of lips when he catches a glimpse of Dave's shirt.

"Hey, fag!" he says. "Who the fuck are you talking to?"

"Huh?" Dave takes him in. A member of Cult of the Shell Necklace. Surprisingly dangerous for white people, these cultists, because they fear nothing. No prisons can hold them, no lawsuits tame them. High school wrestling coaches, the very people administrators look to for discipline, are drawn from their ranks. They're not known for asking rhetorical questions.

"Uhm, Dave."

"Who the fuck is Dave? Your boyfriend? What's his come taste like?"

"I'm Dave. It's me."

"You're Dave!" he bellows. "Hey, Charles," he says, flagging down another cultist, this one sporting, in addition to a shell necklace, the ridiculous white wall haircut (hair on top, dead pale bald scalp around all the sides) that mark him as a member of the warrior caste. "This kid eats his own come!"

Charles likes the sound of that, apparently, and ambles over. My arm feels a ghostly, nostalgic pain.

"I don't," Dave says.

"You calling me a liar, now?" Charles turns and frowns at his friend. Dave sees their sweaters pulse and shift colours with a simmering anger, like the skins of annoyed lizards.

"I think he is."

"I'm not."

"What are you calling him, fag?" Charles demands, with the tips of two thick fingers tapping on Dave's chest. On the still sticky blood.

"Ew, he's got come on him!" Charles exclaims.

"Dude, I can't believe you touched that guy. AIDS test!"

"Dude, shut the fuck up," Charles says. He lifts his hands and hesitates for a second, then grabs Dave by the tops of his shoulders (where there is no blood), spins him around, and twists his arm into a chicken wing.

"You are out, loud, and proud, faggot! Say it!"

"Say what?" Dave says through gritted teeth.

"Say you're a come-eating fag who likes to eat his own come!" suggests the first cultist, almost helpfully.

Dave feels the pain, but it's far off, like his wrist and elbow are twenty, thirty feet away. "I'm a come-eating fag and I like to eat my own come . . . just like you guys do." He gets a book bag to the gut for that, the sharp corner of some overstuffed history text finding rib.

Charles tosses him to the ground, and as if on ritual cue, the first cultist gurgles and sucks loudly, and spits a gob of phlegm and spittle in Dave's hair. They laugh and the pair march off, their arms heterosexually swung over one another's shoulders.

"Eats his own come, that's fucking gross."

"Nobody's eatin' my come but Marni!" says Charles, to ward off evil.

"Aw, she's gotta love that shit."

As they turn the corner, leaving Dave behind in the emptying hallway, Charles recommends to his friend eating pineapple some hours before a date to make one's ejaculate taste sweeter. When they're out of sight, Dave rolls over onto his back and decides that he has lost his taste for Chemistry class. He folds his arms behind his head, crosses his legs and stares up at the ceiling. I'd say something like "time passes" but here in the Ylem it doesn't.

Officer Levine's head comes into view like an unexpected eclipse.

"What are you doing down there?"

"Don't spit on me, please," Dave says, "if you don't like my answer. I'm resting. There was a brutal assault. Can't you see that I'm covered in blood?"

"Get up, you're going down to the office." And he did, and they both did, and there Dave passed Eris, who was leaving as he entered, and she said that he always seems to find himself covered in so many interesting bodily fluids.

Dave sat through the interminable head-shaking lecture by the vice principal, and the filling out of the referral card to the school psychologist, in his tussin haze, but also with an erection.

CHAPTER 3

I never shot anyone, I never did any time, and really I never did much of anything except go to Rutgers, pretend to want to be an architect for two years before dropping out, and end up working for the company that installs New Jersey State Lottery machines in bodegas and liquor stores.

Today I was even back in Jersey City, on the corner of Marin Boulevard and Fourth Street, in a little store in the gentrified area. I never think about high school. I was glad not to be in that part of town. My name, as far as the Filipina woman behind the counter was concerned, was "Broken Yes?" She saved her smiles for the customers, despite the fact that likely half her income was made from the machine I was fixing. Yes, the lottery machine was broken, and I bent over the machine for over an hour, running the usual diagnostic program three or four times, checking the wiring, testing the outside line. In the narrow aisles of the store, near the Chef Boyardee products, a few customers buzzed to themselves and frowned, waiting for me to actually figure out the problem.

"I need to play my numbers," one of them said. An older guy, hard to say whether he was just naturally small or if he'd shrivelled over the years. Drugs. Too much canned spaghetti and forty-dollar dreams. A former Golden Gloves bantamweight boxer who got knocked out in the second round of his first pro fight and was quickly retired by his handlers; with no skills and without the size to be a good bouncer or even a garbage man, he made his way with odd jobs. . . . I do this, making up life stories for the people I encounter. It's a hobby, or a mental problem.

"Well, why don't you go play them at the bodega down the block?"

"No, here. This is my lucky machine."

"Oh?" I said. "Have you won here before?"

"No, but I came very close once. Two numbers on the weekly."

We stared at one another; I was dubious, he was hopeful.

"For three weeks in a row. The past three weeks, I've guessed two numbers right. This week, if I get three numbers, just one more number, bam! Five hundred dollars. This is my week. I'm lucky, I can feel it."

"Well, I'll do my best to finish soon." I looked back down at the guts of the machine and realized that I had entirely forgotten what I was going to try next.

"Smack it on the side, that always works!" Charles said over the sound of the bells tied to the door as he walked in, covered the length of the store in three strides, and opened the refrigerator to retrieve two bottles of Snapple, the fingers of one wide hand wrapping around their necks. He walked up to me and planted himself in front of the lottery machine like it was the cash register on the other hand of the counter.

"C'mon, guy," he said, "give it a good ol' whack." He pantomimed the action with his free hand and smiled. I looked into his eyes; they were blue. I'd remembered them as a deadly sort of brown. He didn't recognize me. God, I felt small just then. Is this how the cashier felt when I looked at her and saw just a tiny birdlike woman with a frown?

Charles laughed at his own joke, because it was even funnier the second time around. Playing along, I slapped the casing on the side of the machine. The sleepy hum of the power source bloomed to activity, and half a dozen receipts worth of paper tongue shot forth from the slit. The dour mood of the place lifted like fog off my glasses; we were all smiles.

"Well, thanks."

"No sweat," Charles said as he shifted over to the cash register and handed over his bottles and a five-dollar bill, expertly slid from a money roll with his thumb. My smile was frozen; however my jaw and cheeks connect to my neck, the tendons had decided to seize up.

"Put the cover on, quick. I need to play my numbers," said the shrivelled man. It wasn't a demand, but the sort of deliriously happy request one might hear from someone who wants to show you the knot of wood that looks just like the Virgin Mary. It was an excuse to turn away from Charles—who was telling me, or everyone else, that he was just here to help—so I replaced the top plate of the casing and snapped it shut.

BULLETTIME

"We are good to go!" The bells jingled again. Charles was gone.

O

I spent almost forty-five minutes in my car, in the parking lot behind the apartment complex next to the store, crumpling, flattening out, then crumpling again the cellophane wrapping my cupcakes had come in. "God, God, I hate myself, I hate everybody, hate myself," I muttered through clenched teeth. My facial muscles still weren't cooperating. I smiled at myself in the rear view mirror. Side view too. "People need to die."

He hadn't even recognized me. I had dreams of that man, dreams where I'd held his lungs in my hands, for years. I wanted to laugh at him because, apparently, he was still stuck in Jersey City while I'd made it out at least to Bergen County. But he was all smiles and good luck, and the lowlifes who hang around mini-marts all day waiting to drop fifty bucks at a time on the Lotto loved him, and I was the fat nerd with black crumbs on his involuntarily gleeful lips who was sitting in his car and looking across the Hudson at the glorious grey skyline of Manhattan where I hadn't even been in three months, not since the little strip mall with the Starbucks and the well-stocked video store had opened across the street from my condo complex.

Maybe he had a shitty job. Hell, maybe he had a great job and owned one of the brownstones they were sandblasting and rehabbing all over downtown. I always wanted to live in a brownstone. Charles was still broad-shouldered. Maybe he was one of those rich contractors working all over the city on spidery scaffolding, shouting at his Latino workers, and then driving home to his McMansion where he has three fat kids with crew cuts or carefully gelled hair who want to go out for junior lacrosse this year, and his wife is happy about that because that means she can shave her pussy again and get some mid-afternoon sex on their white couch under the skylights in their living room bigger than my whole apartment—I was doing it again.

"God, I want to kill," I said again, loud enough to scare myself. I tasted the bitterness in my throat, then smelled it. That weird lemony-herb shampoo Erin's hair always seemed to smell like. Cloves and spittle, I tasted them on my lips like her kiss—everything except pressure and the brush of the tip of her nose against my cheek. The way she would blink.

If the universe worked the way I had thought it did at that moment, it would have started to rain big fat drops, but there was nothing fallacious about this particular pathetic scene, so I just sat there in the fog until the parking lot started filling up as people came home from work in the city. I started my car and drove home with the snack wrappers in my lap the entire way. When I merged onto the freeway, I thought I saw myself sitting in the back seat, a foggy ghost, staring at me with a practiced sneer, but that was only for a second.

CHAPTER 4

Dinner was Kraft Macaroni and Cheese, a flavour I used to miss, but now can taste all the time whenever I like, which is never because I can taste any flavour I like whenever I wish it. I have to say that there is a lot out there most people have never tried. For Dave, the taste of Kraft Macaroni and Cheese is the best part of dinner, which otherwise reminds him of a game of Risk where his forces are being shoved down the cone of South America, isolated in Madagascar, and otherwise utterly destroyed.

His mother, Ann, is "up" as Dave thinks of it, and drinking white wine from a plastic cup; she draws her own pours from the large box sitting on the credenza behind her chair. When Ann is up, she likes to be debriefed by Dave and his father Jeremy, who is a scoop of mayonnaise over a pair of khakis. The dining room—more of a nook formed by the short stem of the L-shaped living room (the kitchen being the space between stems)—smelled vaguely of eucalyptus and burnt chicken, which wasn't helping Dave with his game.

"So, David," Ann says, "I could not help but notice the very large stain on your shirt. Did you not feel the need to change your shirt for dinner?"

Jeremy snorts.

"All my other clothes are dirty—you haven't done laundry in more than a week."

"There's nothing stopping you from doing your own laundry, son," Jeremy says. "I spent a lot of money on that washer/dryer. It's not there to gather dust and hold dirty dishes," he says, swinging an arm toward the kitchen where indeed the top of the washing machine is stacked with dirty dishes, "and I'm sure you can do some dishes once in a while too." Dave opens his mouth to counter that Jeremy can do all those chores just as easily, when Ann outflanks Dave from his left: "And all those dirty shirts are actually still significantly cleaner than the one you're wearing now, aren't they?"

"Yeah—" Dave mumbles, calling time-out by shoving a heaping forkful of macaroni in his mouth.

"You should really do your mother the favour of picking up some of the slack around here," Jeremy says. "Everything is everywhere."

Dave can't argue with that. "Everything *is* everywhere," he repeats.

"Well then, where is my clean house?" Ann asks. She turns to Jeremy. "You can do something once in a while."

"We can all do something; I still think making a spreadsheet with all the chores and our names in three columns, and putting it on the refriger—"

"Bo-ring," Ann says, waving her glass around. Dave sits back in his chair and enjoys scraping some of the crumbly cheese residue from the side of his plate with an artfully forked green bean. He knows he only has a few seconds, as Dad always reacts to Mom's little episodes with the sort of oblivious silence only a man sculpted from mayonnaise can manage.

"This isn't a workplace, Jer," Ann says, then she gulps some wine and holds it in her cheeks while she pivots on her chair to reach her box for a refill. She swallows and continues: "This is a family. We shouldn't need some corporate framework to get our own chores done. We should all be looking to one another"—she looks at Jeremy, then pointedly at Dave—"and thinking, 'What can I do to make my father, or my wife, or my son, more comfortable' because that is what families do. They do things out of love." She stares into space, or at least into the door that leads into the kitchen, for a long moment, then asks without turning back to Dave, "Did you like your dinner?"

"Yes, it's good," Dave says, "thank you for making it."

"That's love!" she says. She points at Dave's dish. "That's love in there. You see, anyone can make macaroni and cheese. I work hard, I want a good meal when I come home. We could go out every night, I could boil lobsters and make fantastic roasts, but I make that, for you, because I know you like it."

Jeremy frowns at the end of his fork. Pasta painted safety orange glistens in the light of the fixture over the table.

Ann gapes. "What do you say about that?" She turns back to Jeremy. Dave wishes Mom would just slide her chair a bit farther back, so she could look at them both at once without having to swing her head like an annoyed snake. Maybe a smaller table would be nice—the long rectangular one the Holbrooks generally eat at reminds Dave of one of those hyperextended cartoon tables with a candelabra and a roasted turkey in the middle.

"He doesn't even know what to say," Jeremy agrees. "Unbelievable. Dave, why can't you just say 'Thank you' to your mother? For dinner? For everything?" His tone is even, like the static between radio stations.

"Thanks, ma," Dave chooses to say, knowing that there is no way to point out that he already thanked his mother without sounding petulant, and petulance is just blood in the water. It doesn't matter. At least they're not talking about his shirt anymore.

"Thanks, ma," Ann repeated. "Well it's too late for 'Thanks, ma' now. These things have to come from the heart, David, the heart. *My* heart is full. Your father's," she says, indicating Jeremy with a slosh of her wine glass, "his heart is full too. Of love. For you. Don't snicker, don't smirk, this is serious. This is the most important thing you'll ever hear in your entire life. I *love* you, David. Your father *loves* you. We do everything for you. This meal, this house, your father's job, every day, every minute, every thought in our lives, David, is oriented toward you because we love you. And all we want in return—no, not even in return because our love for you is unconditional and we'll just keep on loving you no matter what you do or say—but all that we would appreciate is a little appreciation, from the heart. Heart appreciation," she says, that last little bit with a giggle. Her chin sinks to her chest and with a final jerk she is done.

Jeremy sits stoically while Dave stabs repeatedly at the rest of his macaroni and cheese, piling it onto the tines of the fork to gulp it down in a single bite.

BULLETTIME

"So," Jeremy says. "I want an ice cream sandwich. Would you like an ice cream sandwich, Dave? Ann? Ice cream sandwich?" Nobody answers—Ann's unable to, Dave amuses himself by pretending not to hear—and Jeremy says, "Okay, that's three ice cream sandwiches." He pushes his chair from the table dramatically, takes three great strides into the kitchen, collects the ice cream sandwiches from the freezer and walks back. He slides one across the width of the table to a position near Ann, but she doesn't stir, then he forcefully hands one to Dave, who takes it willingly enough.

Jeremy hovers over Dave, holding up the remaining ice cream sandwich and waiting.

"Thanks, Dad," Dave says.

"Yes, yes. That's right. You're welcome, Dave, you're very welcome." Jeremy walks back to his seat, flattens out his crumpled dinner napkin, tears open the wrapper of his ice cream sandwich, and eats it in desperate bites, chewing loudly between them. He's done by the time Dave has his wrapper off, but quickly moves on to Ann's sandwich and polishes that off as well. He stands again suddenly and says good night, causing Ann to stir a bit.

"Clear the table, dear," she mumbles, "clear it, clear it before you go." Then she's back on the sudden nod. Again Jeremy hovers for a moment, then he turns to Dave and says, "You heard your mother; clear the table and start the dishwasher. Carry your weight around here for once."

Dave sits at the table for another two minutes, then leaves without clearing the table or helping his mother to the couch, which he sometimes does when he feels he has won dinner.

Whenever his mother passes by Dave's bedroom and

peers inside, whether during her soporific days or agitated evenings, she declares with a sigh: "Just another average teenage boy's room." Dave hears this in his head and cringes as he goes up to his room, though he knows there is very little average about it. No posters of bikini babes or cars, only teenage boys and middle-aged men take seriously hang from the light blue walls, and there's not a football or baseball to be seen. It's actually pretty neat, except for the ankle-deep sludge of dirty shirts and jeans, the legs all twisted around one another. He heads right to the computer and turns on the monitor with a punch of his finger.

Dave's email client, the web browser, the chat program, the MP3 player, and a couple of the bullshit programs he can't quite be bothered to adjust the preferences on, all compete for resources as they struggle to be the first to start. Dave's scarcely more patient than the computer itself, though it occurs to him that he doesn't actually have anything to do, and isn't waiting on some important email or message. He tries to conceive of what an important email would even be in his case, but can't think of anything. It doesn't matter though; important messages suggest things like deadlines, deadlines imply commerce, commerce means want, and want means the world of the flesh. Not anything Dave is very interested in.

To Dave, the Web was the everywhere he kept everything in. He didn't even feel his fingers hitting the keyboard or manipulating the mouse anymore, but rather felt his self flowing through the monitor, into the net. He laughs, remembering the time his mother dragged herself to the doorway, made her usual comment, and then pointed to the computer to ask if there was any way to get some tax form or another from "in there."

"Not 'In there'," Dave had said. "Out there."

Dave was out there, in the place of all places where music always played, where women splayed their cunts and turned to look over their shoulder, where everyone knew everything about the President and free market and *Star Wars* and "real magic" (with a k!), and where everyone was his friend except for assholes he could blink out of existence with the click of his mouse. Sometimes it took two clicks.

Click. Click.

CHAPTER 5

There were a number of leaflets, photocopies of handwritten material, and print-outs from webpages, blogs, Twitter feeds, Facebook threads, and Bboards in the dossier. One of them read as follows:

RESISTANCE

This is our symbol, this is our hope. All you need to know and all you need to do can be found within its mysteries. Those jagged lines, what are they but a slash and a backslash and a slash and yet another backslash. What is our life, our cause, but an attack followed by our counterattacks, which begets yet another attack, and thus again we counterattack. But the battle ends with us, with our victory!

And what is that symbol but that of a resistor as depicted in a schematic? What do resistors do but sap the power of a circuit, to slow it down and bend it toward new ends? That too is our path and that too is our goal. The power of the system must flow through YOU—prepare yourself (and your Self) and choose your career, your location, your lifestyle. Maximize your impact (the pact between the "I" that is you and the "me" that is all).

And what is the symbol but a set of fangs displayed in a grimace? You must learn to bare your fangs before the system, to intimidate, to threaten, and ultimately to take a bite! Tap into your animal nature, live in the flow of a natural world where freedom is neither means nor ends, but simply the water in which we swim, like a shark in the ocean amidst minnows. We tear through the nets others are trapped in.

To find out more—you know where to look. With-IN.

I put the flyer back down on the table after I finished reading it. My cuffs jingled. My shrink, who sat across from me, asked, "Would you like to talk about what you were trying to say with this, uh, leaflet?"

I laughed. "I wasn't *trying* to say anything. It's said. It's a completed action, a moment in time."

She nodded, pretending to get me.

"And besides, I didn't write it."

"Oh no?"

"I simply inspired it."

"It's signed by you at the bottom, isn't it?"

I laughed—she was such a stupid cunt. "Psychologists are wealthy, aren't they?"

She pursed her lips and played with the eyeglasses that hung from the long necklace of plastic pearls around her neck. She couldn't figure out a way to move the discussion away from where I had decided to lead it, as she knew I'd just "act out" as she liked to call it.

"Some are, some aren't. I'm not, if that's what you're getting at."

"Not very wealthy, but wealthy enough, right? Wealthy enough to get some letter from the President or a Senator, someone who wants your vote and some money, right?"

"Yes, of course. Junk mail."

"Are these letters from the President signed?"

She nodded. What I liked about my shrink, why I didn't just have her taken, to be found three days later in a Wal-Mart parking lot down the shore, the hands of her charred corpse melted to what would be left of her steering wheel. "No, of course not," she said. "A machine signs them, and it's probably some publicist or expert who drafts the letter. They're designed to persuade, even down to the realistic-looking signature."

"Do you consider my signature realistic-looking?" The resistance sigil was repeated at the bottom, in a scraggy, bloody font.

"It is important to you, Mr. Holbrook—"

"Call me *I*!" Snapping gets her attention. I wondered if her father ever hit her. Lots of my girls respond well to snapping because of that. Lots of shrinks enter the field because they want to fix themselves.

"Is it important to you, I, that I think your signature is realistic-looking?" she asked, toneless.

"I do think my signature is realistic-looking," I said, and I chuckled.

"By I, I meant me, you know."

"Yes, exactly."

CHAPTER 6

The next time Dave sees Erin, he is leaning against a billboard on the platform of the cavernous Journal Square PATH station. It really was a cavern cut into the side of a hill—Dave wasn't above thinking of it as "The Batcave," which, to be fair, was what nearly everyone thought the first time they saw it. Dave is daydreaming about that old show from the 1960s (the flame from the Batmobile's rocket engine being used as a weapon somehow, the front wheels smoking and screeching as the car struggled to stay in place while the fire engulfed the side of a criminal hideout) when Erin walks up to the billboard, leans against it next to Dave, winces as her hair is caught between her shoulders and the loud red ad for Hot 97, then steps away to move her long curls over her shoulders, and leans back again. She's wearing a tank top, white, with the words I MOCK YOUR VALUE SYSTEM in black block letters, and denim shorts held up by a brownish belt. Her ass looks a little too big in the shorts, Dave thinks.

"So," Erin asks. "Where are you going?" She hasn't noticed him staring, or, Dave thinks somehow excited by the thought, *She doesn't care if I stare*.

Dave is so smooth. "M-me?"

Erin nods.

He jerks his head away to look down at the platform. It's a newer kind of cement with glittery somethingorothers embedded into the mix. Keeps the cave bright. "The city."

"Yeah, what's in the city?"

He shrugs. "I dunno, everything." Dave glances away.

"But what are you going to do there," she says, her voice developing an edge as she growls the *r* in "there", as she reaches for his hair.

"Ow!"

Erin's eyes flash and she shows her teeth with a wild, jagged smile. Her teeth aren't fixed. "You look at me when I'm talking to you! What the hell is wrong with you?" Dave has never seen such an angry smile.

"Nothing, I'm just going to go—you know, hang out."

"Where?"

"I dunno," Dave says with a shrug. "Around." Her smile is getting even wider—is she cheering up or getting angrier?

"Do you know what stop you're getting off at?" A train was coming. Dave prided himself on knowing on which track a train would arrive from the merest initial vibrations. It was his train this time.

"Uhm . . . Ninth Street. I'm gonna hang out in the Village. You know, look around." Behind Dave, the train rounds the bend to turn into the station from the yard, giving him a chance to shut up. The train slides to a halt in front of them, but the doors don't open.

Dave looks at Erin.

"Look around, eh?" she asks.

"Yeah."

"Exciting stuff! Do you look often?" Dave does look, at the train car nearest them, attempting to open the double doors by force of will. No go.

"So Erin, what brings you to the city?" Erin says to herself aloud.

"Oh, yeah. Uhm, what you going to do in the city?"

"Fuck some strangers," she deadpans. "Not for money or anything. I'm just mad for the cock."

Dave blushes furiously. Erin smiles and slowly raises her hand then points to her shirt. "You're one of those uptight kids, aren't you? I can tell because you're wearing a belt instead of just letting your pants fall past your hips." *But she's wearing one too*, he thinks.

Finally, the doors open. Dave wonders if—and hopes that—Erin will sit next to him, and also that she'll stop being so oddly antagonist. Instead, she sits across from him, across the narrow aisle of the train car. The train moves from the tunnel, and Erin whoops as they hit the sun-drenched elevated tracks. Dave grins as the reddish highlights in her dark mop of hair surface in the light.

"Hey, are you Irish?"

"What?" Erin asks. "What? What the hell is wrong with you!"

Dave slides down in his chair, submissive. "I was just asking."

"I'm Greek. You know, Greek? Ever been to a diner? It's a pleasure to serve you? Tacky murals of the Acropolis? Zorba? Opa? Can't play cards? Big fat weddings?"

"Well your name is Erin—"

"My name's not Erin. That's for you white people. My name is *Irini*," she says, rolling her *r* and elongating her *e*'s to an almost ridiculous extent, at least to Dave's ear.

"Wait, you're white—"

Erin ignores that. "Irini means 'peace'; it's a very common name, actually. After the Greek goddess."

"I never heard of any Greek goddess named Irini." Dave says it "Eye-reenee."

Erin kicks up a sneakered foot, then slams it back down to the floor, coming nowhere near Dave's face, but he flinches anyway. "She's not the sort of goddess you'd find the stats for in your copy of *Deities and Demigods*, but she's real. Oh yes, very real."

Dave leans in, suddenly excited again. "Oh wow, do you RP?" *I'm in*, he thinks.

Erin lifts her hands, "Oh God, forget I mentioned it."

"Well how do you know RPG manuals? Did you have a boyfriend that used to play or something?"

"Oh yeah, I like to fuck strangers who are in college and get good grades—lots of nerds at NYU and Columbia."

"Is that where you're headed now?"

Erin points out the window behind Dave's head. "Ah, is this your stop?"

"Thanks!" Dave says as he hops out of his seat, grabs onto the pole and performs what he hopes is a cool-looking spin toward the opening set of doors, only to be greeted by the sight of a PATH station pillar with a large white letter C on blue tile. Christopher Street. Manhattan's fancy little gay neighborhood, where rainbow flags decorate storefront windows as frequently as stickers for Zagat Guides or the *New York Times*, which is sold everywhere, of course. Flushed, he pivots on his heel and sits back down, while Erin does a little laughing jig in her seat and mouths the word "Fag-got" at him.

His stop, 9th Street, was only twenty seconds away, but they were a long and sullen twenty seconds. Erin stands up with him and loudly calls out, "Bye, David Holbrook of Jersey City who is going to the Village to look around!" as he darts, shoulders lowered and head first, out of the car, through the turnstile, and up the steps and the three-jointed winding tunnel that lets him out on the corner of West 9th and 6th Avenue.

And Dave does look around. He likes the Jefferson Library; its spire and old clock, he decides, look European. It's closed now, though, and sitting on the steps to people-watch is no fun without company. He doesn't like it when the little yappy dogs turn their heads to stare and bark at him while their owners, always imperious and oblivious at once, march down the street without a word of apology. There is a great barrier between Jersey City and Manhattan, despite the PATH train, despite the fact that the Hudson is easily traversable. People from there just don't come here. That's why Dave likes it so much.

Dave decides to walk down to Washington Square Park. He loves the few blocks he traverses; autumn leaves have a smell subtle but pervasive enough to scrub the exhaust out of the air. Brownstones with huge bay windows line the streets, and Dave loves the glimpses of walls painted in tasteful reds, the endless shelves of books, and occasionally on stoops or walking past the windows, the people who can actually, through seniority or million-dollar incomes, afford to live here.

The city, Dave decides, is much different than the

picture painted by his mother's hissing and spitting: "Scum, trash, and spics. The city is a cesspool, a pit. I hate that your father even has to work there," she told him this morning, agitated as she was before her morning tea and palmful of medicine. "Were it up to me, I'd blow up the Holland Tunnel and the PATH train, just to keep the city people from seeping over the river. I don't even know why you want to go there. Just be careful— don't look any black people in the eye. That's how they challenge people on the streets; they'll kill you if you stand up for yourself." He laughed at that, but she was serious, almost frantic, and explained that she had read it in the newspaper once, or maybe it was the TV news, plus she had grown up in Gramercy Park back when New York was at least "half-sane," so she knows what she's talking about. "And don't buy any food from a cart!"

Dave knows plenty about looking down at the ground when confronted anyway, but walking to the park, which is easy enough to find, he holds his chin high and smiles. He doesn't even wonder what this would feel like on cough medicine till he gets to the crowded park and hangs out on the fringes of several knots of NYU students who play guitars, bullshit in the shade under trees, or fall off their skateboards and gamely get up to try again.

Dave is too shy to talk to anyone, and is for once glad of his power of near-invisibility. He loves walking lazy circles around the fountain and the larger concentric circles of the park's paths, flowing from the rapid-fire hip-hop of someone's freestyling ("I'll cap yo' ass like a motherfucker/pump the bass like a motherfucker/go to class learn a rhyme for motherfucker . . . motherfucker!") to an old man's violin—Dave throws seventy-five cents in quarters into the case at the man's feet—to the strum of a guitar and the enthusiastic warbling of some minor Beatles tune. It's sunny. Lots of girls are out, most of them casually chatting and leaning in close toward one another, the way girls do, and showing off the straps of their thongs, all for Dave. Robitussin would make that last more convincing, he thinks.

He buys an expensive Coke and an outrageous pretzel from a cart, shuffles through a flock of pigeons, sending them flying, and is drawn to the dog run by the dusty tussles and barking. Surrounding the park like barbed wire, the properties of New York University, some of them gutted brownstones, others modern buildings of slab concrete and eight-foot-high windows. Dave wants to go to NYU; then he can come to the park and actually know the people here, have something to talk to them about, like organic chemistry or Free Mumia. (A band? Is reggae cool? He makes a mental note to download some when he gets home.) He sneaks the last chunk of his pretzel through the wire fence and watches a smiling Lab mix run to him and snag the treat whole. He wonders if he'll see Erin in the park; maybe she really does fuck strangers. Everyone out here sure seems friendly with one another, the way they sit so close even in the heat, or cuddle in the shade of the trees. Maybe he could even find a girl who likes to fuck strangers, if he only knew how to identify them and what to say.

Dave realizes he's pacing after he passes the same chess game four times, and decides to find some place to eat. He cuts down Washington Square Park South and walks in the valley of row houses and tasteful little stores, heading deeper into the Village. Everything looks kind of expensive, or at least French; even little luncheonettes with room for only two tables seem to pride themselves on foreign-seeming signage and weird foods. Like pad Thai and Orangina. Dave suddenly wonders how many of the guys back in the park were gay; did they think he was looking for a pick-up or hustling or something with all his obvious walking around by himself?

He blushes, makes a right, and comes along a more soothing street. It has a McDonald's on it, like an oasis. He didn't come all this way to eat a Value Meal #2 though, and even McDonald's is a buck more across the Hudson, so he decides on the small diner three doors down. It's not a big chrome and tin job like he's used to from Jersey, but the Washington Place Diner And Restaurant (Two rooms? Two menus?) looks inviting enough, with booths and a counter and even a revolving display case full of fluffy cakes and almost menacing-seeming pies. The door is wide open and exhaling nicely chilled air-conditioned air as well, and Dave can almost smell the grease of the disco fries in the air. He walks up the steps and into the vestibule, and through the second glass door separating the foyer from the diner proper (or is this the restaurant section?), he sees her.

She's behind the counter, a white button-up shirt and black blazer over her tank top, lifting a plate smeared with ketchup and the leftover lettuce and coleslaw of a Burger Platter Deluxe with one hand and wiping down the Formica under it with her other. He stays long enough to watch her shove the plate across the stainless steel shelf under the window that separates counter from kitchen, walk back to the counter to pocket her buck and change tip, and then take up her position, bored-looking, arms crossed, with an empty frown on her face, by the cash register. Behind her, and behind the soda fountain, and the short-order cook who stands out, as he's a black man, Dave sees the faded blue skies and crumbling pillars of a tacky mural of the Acropolis.

Dave turns and runs back the two blocks to the PATH train and stands on the mostly empty platform for nearly half an hour before the train going back to Jersey comes, smoldering in an inexplicable shame.

CHAPTER 7

The Ylem isn't so much a place as it is the canvas places are painted on. Here I can live every decision and detail of an infinite number of me. Of course the shooting cuts a huge red slash through my personal Ylem, like a line in the financial pages after a stock market crash. Sometimes I was able to resist Eris for weeks, or months, before pulling the trigger. A couple of times she never got to me at all.

There are endless realities shifting and swirling in the Ylem, and I've lived them all. Nothing else to do, really. I died a baby due to bronchitis, and never felt anything more than cold and a harsh thimble full of air. There was an "accident"—that's what the principal called it—in eighth grade. I was accidentally cornered and kicked so hard in the ribs that splinters of bone tore right through my guts. I didn't even die till seventh period, in World Literature.

I never live past forty. No matter what, I never marry. No kids. Sex sometimes, in college, thanks to beer and a sad little aura of being the nicest guy in some ramshackle dorm at Stockton College. That me studied psychology. The school was close to Atlantic City, so I learned to count cards and I didn't need to work, as long as I lost frequently enough to keep the Mafia from beating me up in an alley. I learned that trick from some guy I met in an alley. Later, I die in a car wreck.

Those are the boring lives. Most of them are very boring, with nothing more to say for them than a really good meal, or a glimpse in the dark of a dazed smile on the face of a pretty girl I managed to get into bed and make come.

Eris is like a pillar of flame, splashing heat and light all across the narrow hallways of my life's labyrinth. And she put me here, to make me her slave.

I'm not Dave Holbrook; I'm just the part of Dave Holbrook who wasn't insane. She had so many ways and so many tricks; in the Ylem I see them all very clearly, and while poor lost Dave twists and writhes against a million predestinations, like a prisoner being prodded to the lip of a grave at bayonet point, at the crack of a whip, from the tug of a leash around his neck. Eris is truly a goddess. It's scary to see free will in action. They control the rest of us. If they're flame, we're moths.

She ignores Dave in the halls and in the classroom. Dave walks through his days in a soporific stupor, too blitzed to notice even when Malik holds out a big meaty arm for Dave to walk into, sending him to the floor. Malik laughs, then yawps when his laugh doesn't compel a sufficient number of girls to turn around. Then he walks on. There's no rhyme or reason for these attacks, and that's what they are, Dave decides. There isn't some group of students who are bullies or gang members or "acting out," however people put it—attacks and assaults come in waves. It's information, abstract, that occasionally finds a medium of expression in someone next to Dave.

A chop to the throat, light but painful enough, then some big brown eyes in his face, demanding this or that admission of joy in taking it up the ass like a fag, or in being a white dick-eating bastard. Dave mutters some response, and the mouth under the eyes says, "Excuse me?" But it's not arrogant, or threatening, or a simmering response to a perceived challenge, the kid—whatever his name was, James something—really just said, "Excuse me?" the way his mother must have taught him to do at age three whenever he didn't hear something completely.

Erin walks by, a magazine folded over in her left hand, her eyes squinting (Dave finds the hint of crow's feet attractive, a flaw that makes her accessible) and Dave shouts in the hope that she'll turn around. "I said fuck you! You're the faggot!"

Dave's nose crunches under a fist, Erin turns a corner, blood wells up in the undersides of Dave's eyes. The pain feels like it's four feet away, and to the left.

James (his name was James) is suspended for a week and no more because Dave shouted and that means it was a fight between kids and not a random assault, and besides, as James explained, yeah he threw the fist but it was Dave's nose that broke and he had no idea such a thing could happen because his punch was more of a tap. Dave's week is spent with Ann discovering the injury anew every morning—"Are your eyes *still* red? When are the bandages coming off again?"—and Jeremy just frowns and asks whatever happened to those Tae Kwon Do lessons Dave had two summers in a row when he was eight and nine.

And Erin walks by. Erin hops the turnstile at the PATH station and flips off the shouting janitor, while Dave stands at the top of the escalators, staring till he gets an elbow to his back. Erin walks by while Dave eats a Philly cheese steak in the food court at the mall (he's waiting for his movie to start; he goes in the afternoon because it's cheaper and he can go alone with a minimum of hassles), and she's the only female he sees that isn't clutching at least two heavy-looking bags of boring mall store clothing. Erin walks by in dreams and in dreams Dave has some witty line to share but the floor warps and collapses into the Ylem and I flail into the darkness—but how it really happened involved the one time Erin didn't just walk by.

Erin walks into Dave's room while he sits playing some flash game on the computer and she says, "Hi!" like a friendly eight-year-old making a new friend on the playground. Dave yelps and jerks around, his chair teetering. They hadn't said a word to one another since the day he saw her working at the diner. Dave hadn't even been to the city since then.

"Your mother let me in. I told her that we're studying together." Erin smiles. "I even told her that it was for the Health class unit on Human Sexuality, and I brought a visual aid." She shrugs her backpack off her shoulder, reaches into it and withdraws a diapered five-pound bag of flour. Hefting it in her palm, her lips pursed from the tiny strain, she says, "Catch," and lobs it underhanded to Dave, who grunts and nearly fumbles as the flour thumps hard against his chest and hiccups a puff of white powder.

"You're the worst father ever!" Erin shrieks, her hands clawing her hair. Dave twitches and more flour spills as Erin slides back into her smirk, and with a hand cupped to her ear pantomimes listening closely for footsteps or a motherly holler from downstairs, but nothing is forthcoming. "She must be sleeping it off, the poor dear," Erin says. Then she shuffles across the room, dragging dirty clothes along her ankles, and plops onto the bed. Dave holds the bag of flour in his lap and looks at her, glances at his monitor, then looks at her again.

"Whatcha up to?" she asks. "Cybersex?"

He blushes. "Homework." Then the computer sings a downbeat song of defeat.

"Ah, your *Battle Station Mars* homework. You are a scholar and a gentleman, even if you are an abusive father."

"Uhm." A steady stream of flour puddles by his feet. "Erin? Why are you here? We're not even in Health this semester, and I've only ever seen this flour thing on TV."

"Yeah, that's where I got the idea from too. Why do you think the school district doesn't want us to have flour? Do you think people would sneak cocaine into the schools?"

"Erin—"

"Or guns! Handguns in the flour. Do you think there are a lot of guns in school, Dave? I'm very nervous. I hate my parents for moving out here."

"Where are you from, anyway?"

"Will you protect me from the gangs, Davey?" Erin pleads. Then she laughs at him, not even bothering to pretend to laugh with him. Dave briefly considers the immense psychosocial, linguistic, intersubjective, and formal determinants of whether one is laughing with or at someone and whether he can actually know what Erin's doing since she is so obviously crazy and probably on drugs herself, but he puts all that aside and just says, "Maybe you should protect me from them. I don't even think anyone's in a gang, really. I mean, gang members are busy during the day and stuff; they have no time to learn about the American Revolution."

Erin is serious, like the face on a nickel. "Could you really use some protection?" She smiles and leans back, shifting subtly to make the bottom of her shirt rise, showing off a bit of tummy.

"Well, not from you—"

"Oh, you already have some protection, I see." She's not smiling. "Can I see it?"

"What are you talking about?" Dave is flushed, sweating, actually trying to make himself annoyed and humiliated enough to gain some sort of upper hand. The bag of flour in his lap is a small blessing. "Small blessing." *Christ, I thought like my mother, and that was without any cough syrup—but she won't even let him have that.* "Drop the bag, come over here and sit next to me on your bed," she says and he does, so eager for something.

She turns to him and says, "I have a proposition for you. And no, that doesn't mean I'm propositioning you." This he laughs at half-authentically; it sounds like the sort of wordplay a sophisticated person would appreciate, so he tries to. She touches his wrist like in the movies, but he should be doing it, he knows, and the knowledge burns in his cheeks.

"Let's you and I," Erin says, her tongue an eel, "form a secret society. Just the two of us. Tell nobody."

Dave asks, "Who would I even tell?" and imagines trying to explain all of this to Oleg—that guy who wears a fedora every day—and Erin says, "Aren't you friends with that fedora guy?" and Dave says, "Not really," and Erin says, "Good."

"We'll communicate in code. Meet secretly. Make plans. Learn to read one another's thoughts. Chart the course of world events, eventually, with the school as a test of concept." Erin reaches out and Dave waits for a kiss, paralyzed, but she stretches past him to take hold of a blanket piled up at the corner of the bed. She gives it a dramatic magician yank and smiles as it fills the space before the bed and gently eases to the floor.

"The initiation is simple. I will entirely remake your personality to better serve the needs of the collective, and through a lifetime of praxis you shall achieve *theosis*, or knowledge of God." Erin holds up two corners of the blanket she had spread out.

Dave giggles and says, "Sure, lay it on me!"

Erin rolls her eyes and sighs. "You are a fucking idiot, you know that." Then she swings the blanket over Dave's head and covers him with it, then whips it off with a practiced movement and I go screaming into the Ylem, trapped for what seems like eternity, but what is really just an endless moment. What's left of me in that dumpy bedroom in the unfolding universe is the Dave who cannot help but obey.

CHAPTER 8

Erin tackles him and gives his lips a lick with the very tip of her tongue, then rolls off him and out the door. Erin rises up like a snake and shifts out of her shirt, then grabs Dave by the sides of his head to drag his mouth up to her body; she stays and they fuck clumsily on Dave's sagging twin bed. Erin stays on her corner of the bed, folding the blanket in her lap and mumbling about her parents—their ridiculous demands, Old World expectations (no dating, work work work, Christmas in January), and her father's regular thundering at the TV, over tax bills, at the Puerto Rican busboys down at the diner. Erin teaches Dave several lines from *The Iliad*, or says that they're from the poem—and an important part of his initiation—but they were really just a string of modern Greek curses: *Gamo ton shisto bou s'eshese*, she says, and he proudly repeats in an ancient sing-song, "I fuck the pussy that vomited you out." It doesn't matter which choices she made, Dave was hers regardless. I love to live through his eyes as her belly and shoulders roll over him; over and over I replay her solemn little talk, wondering if this time she'll cry, or admit that it's all lies. Never happens.

I can be anywhere Dave ever was, in any of the streams of his life, of *my* life. It's hard to remember, especially as I stand over his body, tucked and curved into itself like a fetus in his own blood and urine, his last rattling breath still hanging in the air amidst the whimpers and the moans of the wounded. Once, a kid, a sensitive little guy named Ray who liked trip-hop and weed, caught a glimpse of me—me, standing over my own stained corpse—through the chicken wire and papier-mâché of the world. He shrieked and ran.

"I saw that guy. You know, that dude! He was standing over another guy who looked just like him," Ray explained to his crew of friends who had already grown bored with Hacky Sack.

They were a smear of baggy black clothing, clownish makeup, and whiteboy dreads, and they didn't believe him, despite their steady diet of Wiccan paperbacks from the New Age section of the B. Dalton at the mall. "Bullshit," they said. The ones with a bit of a rep for being tough or especially magically powerful among their cohort—they bought their books from the real pagan shops in the city—made their pronouncement like it was two words. "Bull. Shit."

But they all went to go stare at the corner between their classes, and a couple of them were even sure they saw me, though I was actually standing behind them. Ray's story sounded much better when Ray wasn't the one telling it. "Oh man, I *totally* saw that guy. It was like he was crying over his own body—like a guardian angel who failed."

BULLETTIME

The corner has a chill attached to it. Can't you feel it?

It smells like blood and steel here. It smells like the streets did on the afternoon of 9/11, when the wind shifted and carried the dust of the ruins over the river. I can taste it on my tongue, like I could when the shooting began.

In an hour the school was united in gleeful horror over the idea of the dead white guy haunting the place. The district even sprang for an extra counselor for a week or two. The vice principal got online and sold the story anonymously to one of the tabloids for five grand, then bragged about it to everyone in the faculty lounge, then realized that the money barely covered the outstanding debt on one of his credit cards and shut up about it. The school had a closet built into the corner where Dave died. It's a little eerie, even to me, to stand in the middle of the leaning mops and the sparkling jeers of various cleaning product logos and mascots, waiting for the door to open at the crack of dawn.

Experiencing Dave's body—the one crumpled on the third floor of Hamilton High School, that is—feels like crawling into the slice left by cleaning and gutting a fish: cold, slimy, and ridiculous. When Dave wins, on the other hand, when those years of *Dungeons and Dragons* mapmaking pay off, when love and rage fill his heart like battery acid, and when he walks down the steps of his school all giddy and his arms heavy and hot from the shootings, that's like stepping into an orgasm and riding it like a cab down a glorious spring day street. The day The Resistance is born.

Then there are the endless Daves who don't do it at all—the ones who stand outside the school, lips torn and bleeding, who turn around and go back home. Then ones

57

whose plans melt like dirty slush the closer it gets to E-Day; a dozen Daves just live the fantasy of murder over and over as they shoulder and squeeze their way down Newark Avenue during lunch period—if only there was a way to clear the streets in a moment; point the gun and let the bodies bloom like instant red roses.

Their bodies are all like dead fish too, if not in high school then by college. Communications major, Business Admin minor, nine credits of Japanese—maybe we'll get into anime translation/localization or something, but we drop out or shuffle into Dad's office or end up pushing around overhead projectors in the DoubleTree Hotel by the mall. We buy used Hondas because they're sensible and worlds away from the awesome crime-fighting vehicles we used to design with crayon and construction paper. Our girlfriends have high Jersey hair and dull blue eyes and generally find us on the rebound from some five-year relationship with a barrel of a man named Ted or Bryant. They leave quickly enough too, after a summer of somedays about trips to Paris or marriage or moving out to some place where the houses have nice lawns and the Puerto Ricans are all cleaning ladies.

Then there is the Kallis Episkipos. He lives in exile in another world, say his followers, despite the claims of the media and law enforcement and no, they don't mean me. This is the Dave who walked out of Hamilton with raw trigger fingers and an eagerness to eat JCPD bullets from the cordon around the entrance, the one locked up variously in prison or mental hospitals, and his leaflets, zines, and broadcast email broadsides. The kid who got his nose sliced open with a shiv twenty minutes into his sentence and returned the favour that night by gouging out the eyes of his attacker—and replacing them with a pair of blue robin's eggs he had somehow smuggled into prison. He dreamed of murders and got those dreams into the hands of fat girls from Ohio. You know, the ones with the long hair to cover their faces and the black blogs with purple lettering, and the box cutters to the throats of their ridiculous high school enemies. ("She called me a slut, once." "I'm half-Jewish and he told me that God didn't love me. And he was right, but Kallis Episkopos does.") The man who after his death had an entire issue's worth of *The Journal of Police and Criminal Psychology* dedicated to articles about him and the movement he sparked.

Sliding into him is like living in an alcoholic who can taste the Jack Daniels on her tongue in every glass of juice or soda, right before she finally says, "Fuck it," and marches out to get laid, get drunk, and get royally fucked by the world she's determined to toss herself out in front of. Kallis Episkipos is Dave Holbrook, with free will reclaimed.

And me? I'm Dave Holbrook too—where Kallis Episkipos has free will, I have no will at all, no way to affect the world or my own life. But I get to see it all; every moron mistake and anguished inevitability. Somewhere along the infinite planes of the Ylem, there must be a way out, a way to live and a choice to make that frees us from the grip of Eris, that frees me from this waiting room of raw experiences. I just need to find it.

CHAPTER 9

Dave isn't surprised to find himself bleeding again. He is prepared even, and seals shut the pen-made wound in his belly with his handy tube of Krazy Glue. Dave had never even seen the kid in school before, but he had heard that he was somebody's cousin or something, from Newark, where the shit that happened was always a lot fucking heavier than in Jersey City.

"Shit shit shit shit shit," he seethes through cable-tight teeth. He pinches the flab—Dave was a skinny kid with a paunch, the worst of both worlds—with his blood-smeared left hand and applied the glue with the right, then held the wound shut. He doesn't need stitches—he wouldn't *get* stitches anyway. Half a roll of toilet paper is just enough blotter for his injury, his hands, the streaks and drips around the bowl, and the walls of the far stall in the second floor boy's room, all of which he'd managed to get pretty sticky when he ran in here, book bag and windbreaker flying. The toilet is jammed tight with crumpled red and purple toilet tissue; they float like a mass of abstract origami flowers.

Dave sits still as he can, breathing through his mouth—the floor smells like piss and Ajax—and waits for the glue to set. A comically oversized cock and balls, fireworks shooting forth from the tip, decorates the stall door. "Well," Dave says to himself, "fuck."

Outside the stall, a pair of boots, black with thick and useless buckles on the side, march up to and stop before the door. The dusty leather of a trench coat drags behind them. Dave cringes.

"Hail!" says a voice, half-strangled between adolescence and the deep baritone of adult blowhards, on the other side of the door.

"*Occupado*, Tigger," Dave says.

"I know that," Oleg says. "Why would I greet an empty bathroom stall?"

"Because you're crazy? I dunno. Look, I don't want to talk right now."

"I couldn't help but notice a suspicious-looking trail of blood leading right to the door here—"

"Yeah yeah, I know, listen, I'm fine—"

Oleg wasn't the sort to allow himself to be interrupted; in fact Dave knew he was just the sort of asshole who'd simply start over again even if his question had already been answered, and he did: "I couldn't help but notice a suspicious-looking trail of blood leading right to the door here—" Dave sighs, but lets him finish, "and I was wondering if you might be in need of any assistance."

"I said I was fine, didn't I?" Dave says.

"Indeed you did, but I have evidence that you're not actually fine."

The glue sets. Dave reaches up, shifts the bolt of the little lock, and gingerly pushes open the door. Oleg grins widely, like he had just turned to the centrefold in some porno mag. Dave wishes he could kick high enough to knock the fedora off Oleg's mop of frazzled hair.

"So, you think you can help?" Dave says, nasty like his mother. That edge in the voice.

"Actually," Oleg says, punching each syllable—ack chew ah lee—like the word was new to him, "I believe that I can." He snaps the rim of his trench coat and squats to meet Dave's glassy eyes. "I think it's past time we taught some of the dirtbags in this school a lesson."

Dave laughs and laughs. "Oh gawd. What are you going to do? Teach me to kill people with mind bullets?"

Oleg folds his arms over his chest and scowls, trying to look intimidating in his long coat, but he barely manages rumpled. "I'm not the one bleeding," he says. "Maybe I have resources you lack."

Dave brings the glue stick to his nose and inhales deeply, then mocks: "Maybe I have resources you lack," he says, his chin against his collarbone, his voice an octave deeper than usual. Dave props himself up with his elbow and the rim of the toilet, winces, and falls again. Oleg reaches down to help Dave to his feet.

"Thank you, Tigger," Oleg says.

"Thank you, Tigger," Dave repeats.

The door to the boy's room bangs open and the whooping and howling begins. "Hey, they're in the stall together!" Lee announces to nobody, his smile wide like a horse's. "Suckin' cock, no doubt." Dave steps out of the stall and stands next to Oleg, his mouth a scribbled line. "Damn, you're bleeding again, guy," Lee tells him.

Dave walks up to Lee, beelining for the door, almost hoping for a standoff, but Lee steps out of the way and raises his hands. "Uh oh, AIDS blood comin' through," he says as Dave strides tall into the hallway. The door closes, Dave's knees buckle, his hands move to his wound, and around the corner comes Vice Principal Fusco. In the muffled distance, Oleg squeals, "Hey quit it!" and Lee laughs. The fedora rolls on its sharp edge out of the bathroom and into the hall. For a moment, all is a blur.

". . . and this time, I was just," Dave says, "poked."

"Poked?" Fusco is a small mountain behind his overburdened desk. Dave doesn't know many men with beards, he realizes. Fusco's white whiskers suggest Santa Claus and the precision of some laser-guided razor available only via late-night TV infomercials at the same time. "With what?"

"A shiv."

"What do you mean, 'a shiv'?" Fusco's hands are up, his fingers twitching around the word.

"A pen."

Fusco takes a note: "A penknife."

"No, just a pen."

"Just a pen. First you bit your tongue, then you were stabbed—"

"Poked."

"—with a pen."

"Yes."

Fusco says, "It's not been a very good year for you so far, Mr. Holbrook, has it?"

Dave shrugs.

"Who is—" Fusco glances down at some notes, "'Tigger'?" The hands shoot up again. Dave swallows a chuckle and winces from the glued stitch in his side.

"Oleg Broukian."

"Is Tigger some sort of gang name?"

Dave can't help but laugh at that, but shudders from the pain. "Heh, no. He calls himself Tigger because the wonderful thing about tiggers is that he's the only one."

"What on Earth is that supposed to mean, Mr. Holbrook?" Fusco asks, a volcano rumbling.

"Honestly, I have no idea. But I've met, like, three Tiggers online, and they all say that they're the only one."

"So," Fusco says, "you spend a lot of time 'surfing the web,' do you?" His fingers go up and the conversation descends into hell. Parents are called, and in my old home Ann sleeps through fifty-seven rings. She always hated answering machines. Oleg's folks actually show up, looking like fire plugs that had eaten other fire plugs, and hustle their son away. His hair waved in strands on the breeze as he was pushed by meaty shoulders and clasping hands into a grey beater Volvo. Nurse Alvarez comes and frowns at the Krazy Glue holding together the slice of skin on Dave's stomach, while Fusco in the other room harrumphs at the district attorney over the phone.

"He should go to the hospital," the nurse tells Fusco.

"I'm not going," Dave says.

"Yes you are."

"No he's not," Fusco calls out from the interior of his office. "We can't send him anywhere without parental permission." He walks out and looks at Alvarez. "Except home. Which we will—" he turns as if he had been practicing with a mirror in the other room "—for one week. You're suspended, Mr. Holbrook."

Dave starts, then winces again. Alvarez puts a hand on his shoulder. Tamed, Dave asks as calmly as he can (though his hands are clenched into fists; he hopes the stance will pass as pain and not rage). "Why am I being suspended? What did I do? What about the guy who stabbed me?"

Fusco raises an eyebrow. "I thought you said you were poked."

"Either way, I'm the victim," Dave says, teeth clenched.

"You're a victim in one sense," Fusco says, "but not in every sense. We have rules, insurance liability, standards of behaviour. Plus, we don't know who attacked you. 'Italian-looking African-American' . . . I don't even know what that's supposed to mean—" here went the fingers again, "—'someone's cousin,' doesn't really cut it. We do know, however, that you brought contraband, the Krazy Glue, which might be an inhalant, into the school, and then used it inappropriately."

Alvarez rises from her crooked posture and says, "Damnit, just take the week off. It's a vacation. I can use a week's vacation too."

"I left a message with your parents. Three, in fact. When do they come home?"

Dave stands. "My mother's probably already home. Do I get a police escort or an ambulance ride too?"

"If you can't walk, I'll drive you home, Holbrook."

Dave can walk. Dave walks out of the main office, down two flights of wide marbled steps and into the early autumn afternoon. The street is bare of the usual bustle of classmates that accompany lunch or dismissal. Dave almost feels like a real live human being for a moment, the sort of person who can go into a store and buy something, or look at a tree and appreciate it as he strolls by. Then like a breeze Erin appears beside him, takes the crook of his arm in hand, and without saying a thing leads him away from school, away from home, and down Newark Ave. Under their feet a Conrail train pulling a dozen tanker cars rumbles past and sends pigeons flying by the swarm.

CHAPTER 10

Even back in the days of swilling cough medicine, I'd tell myself that at least I wasn't going to end up being one of those guys who peaked in high school. That's probably why the version of Dave I found most interesting was the one who did just that. His life was like watching a glacier melt. He was also one of the only ones who kept in contact with Ann instead of running, screaming, away from her. Actually, he still lived with her, in Bergen County. Jeremy died of an early heart attack, thanks to a congenital condition. Nothing so melodramatic as an insane alcoholic wife and a failure of a son took him down.

I never got used to my mother. She changed. When I was a kid, she was a dreamy drunk. A murmurer and forgetter. But something had turned, even before Dad's death. The wine in her had fermented into a sour vinegar. And she couldn't take care of herself, so I had to take her in. I'd stay out late after work, and she'd shriek at me till the neighbours called the police. Or I could come right home after work, but that would just mean a slower boil and an earlier climax. I tended to split the difference, rolling in around eight.

I liked the video store near my home. It had parking in the back—I always imagined it was for porno fans who didn't know how to use the Internet—and the employees were always happy to see me. They were contractually obligated to smile and make conversation. Not like those Starbucks bitches, who marched us customers through the line like we were prisoners being deloused.

I wasn't the sort of person so desperate for human attention that I flirted with every female retail employee I encounter. *Hey, Mindy! Heh heh, yeah, you have a nametag. I guess we're on a first-name basis. . . .* Mindy really was very into movies. She kept good ones in reserve for me. Netflix can't do that. Not nearly as well, anyway. She was a mousy girl. Mid-20s. No college for her because her folks were poor and she was unenthusiastic in school. Small boobs, like someone who used to be an athlete. Good smile, okay teeth. Doable, but . . .

I was sure she had a similar summary of me—chubby guy with glasses. Jewish nose. Works for the state. Doesn't know how to make a machine spit out a winning lottery ticket. Lives with his mother, but only because she's crazy, or so he says. Not doable.

Thus my but.

"Dave!" Mindy was excited to see me. I always tense when people call my name in public. After all these years, I still worry that someone will overhear my name, then follow me around and shout it at me. But the store was empty save for Mindy and a pair of teens looking over the videogames, and me. She reached under the counter and produced a DVD. "This is the one. Wong kar-wai's *2046*."

"Sci-fi?"

"Uhm . . . kinda." Mindy got quiet. She didn't want to be known as the type of girl who watches sci-fi films. "I mean, there are different timelines and stuff. There's a sci-fi story wrapped up in the other stuff. And it's non-chronological."

"Hmm, sounds good." I picked up the DVD case and made a show of considering it. I really just wanted to ask Mindy to come home with me and watch it on my couch. But my mother would be on the couch, silently stewing. "Is this subtitled?" Subtitles put my mother to sleep, which is half the reason why I became a cinephile.

"Yeah, of course," Mindy said.

"So," I said, "not a good movie to have on while making out on the couch, right?"

Mindy blushed. "Well . . ." Then her face changed. "Don't you live with your mother? Ha ha, you'd better not be making out on the couch, right?"

"Yeah, right." If only the whole world and everyone in it would die, right now. A gigantic solar flare would be sufficient. My own spine was already boiling. "Can't have that. Uhm, I'll take it. But I want to look around first too."

"Sure, okay," Mindy said. "I'll be here."

I'll be here. What did that mean? It was flirty, certainly. Now I had to find another DVD, and one that would impress Mindy. Not another foreign film though—that would be too obvious. Indie, but not too recent. Anything with Parker Posey in it was disqualified. Then I found it—*Ghost Dog*. Masculine, yet thoughtful. Everyone with half a brain loves Jarmusch. And it was filmed in Jersey City, so I had another conversational gambit in hand when I got back to checkout.

"You like this movie, eh?" Mindy said.

"Sure, don't you?"

She tapped the screen with a fingernail. She kept them long, but they weren't ridiculously so, and she didn't paint her nails. Just feminine enough. I liked that. "You've rented it three times. We have used copies if you want to own it."

"Nah, that's all right. So . . ."

"Hmm?"

"Well?"

"Hmm-hmm?" She raised an eyebrow and smiled at me.

"Do you like *Ghost Dog*?"

"I'm more of a *Night on Earth* girl," she said.

"Winona Ryder!"

Mindy said, "And those Helsinki guys."

We'd run out of steam so I blurted out, "Part of why I like *Ghost Dog* is because it was shot in Jersey City. I grew up there."

"Cool."

"Ever been?" I asked.

"To Jersey City?" Mindy said. "Well, no. I mean, except on my way to the Holland Tunnel."

"Haha, that was the local joke. 'What is there to do in Jersey City?' 'Go to New York.'"

"Do you spend a lot of time in New York?"

"Not as much as I'd like, Mindy." *Say her name*, I thought. *Use the name*. "Do you? Do you ever go to the Film Forum or stuff like that?"

"Not as often as I'd like to." She smiled again.

"Yeah, well I bet working here till 10 p.m. most nights puts a real crimp on social activities, eh?" I practically saw the words hanging in the air between us, like a small cloud of pollution. I'm an idiot.

"Yeah," Mindy said, her voice flatlined.

"Well, see you," I said. What was that line from that short story? *Gazing up into the darkness I saw myself as a creature driven and derided by vanity; and my eyes burned with anguish and anger.* Except instead of darkness it was a well-lit parking lot.

Mother wasn't interested in movies, or in much of anything. She never asked me how my day went, or what I was up to. Instead, there was a monologue. "On *Wheel of Fortune* tonight, the phrase was 'Clam Digger' and the only letter missing was the 'D.' And the dopey contestant guessed, 'N.' Can you believe that? Pat Sajak looked about ready to shit himself," she began as I walked in.

"Wow, that's messed up. Hi, Mom," I said, but she didn't stop. She didn't follow me into the kitchen or even raise her voice or anything like that. I'm not the type of man to drink beer or wine after work, not with the negative example of Ann on the living room couch every day, but I found three Oreos and poured myself a glass of water.

"—fourteen-point air-conditioning system. And you know I hate when the phone rings, it just drives me up the wall."

"You can always turn the ringer off," I said as she kept talking.

"So I asked what the fourteen points were. All fourteen. I said, 'Go on, list them for me.' And then I had

71

a question about each one of them. I kept him on the phone for seventy-five minutes before telling him that I rent—"

"That *I rent*. You mean *I* rent."

"And, I have to say, the kid was real professional. I could barely hear him gritting his teeth." Then mom was nearly done. "Oh, I'm so tired. Davey, baby, could you . . ." She trailed off, but looked longingly over to the box of wine on the dining room table we never used. Her glass was in her hand, empty, and she raised her arm like a dying silent movie star. Of course, I gave her her refill.

"We'll need more later. It's almost empty."

"We have another in the pantry."

"No, I don't think we do . . ." Then, "Shhh, *Dateline NBC* is on."

"God, that show's always on."

"We don't have any more in the pantry. You think I don't know what's in my own pantry?" She gulped wine. I ate two cookies whole and went to my room to watch the DVD on my TV. It was good, though I admit to being bored enough and horny enough to get on the Internet and trawl one of the bondage servers on IRC. I'm not a freak or anything, but it's where older guys can talk to college girls who like taking cameraphone shots of themselves in nothing but thongs. Or maybe collegeslut420 really is an older guy who once got a teen girl to strip, and he's just spreading the joy in disguise. LOL, as they say, lol. The trick is to keep from getting wrapped up in conversations with fifty-five-year-old "BBW"s looking to escape into the world of sensual spankings.

Mindy, Jesus. That's who I jerk off to, despite the oceans of porn.

CHAPTER 11

Erin has a knack for first aid. "I had to sew my father up once," she explains, a needle in her mouth. "Crazy guy wanted to take the cash register, and he had a machete." They're in the apartment Erin lives in with her parents. It's a ramshackle railroad apartment, but Erin has her own entrance and a shoebox-sized room. It's the first girl's room Dave's ever been in. He's surprised—no posters, no stuffed animals. Piles of clothes everywhere. "Papa has the huge slash in his arm. Totally brutally mangled," she says.

"Really?" Dave is shocked. Erin pinches his skin hard and he writhes under her grip. There's pain now.

"No, not really. I'm a friggin' pathological liar," Erin says. "Aren't you glad I'm doing minor surgery on you?"

Dave thinks the glue was fine and says so. Erin snorts. "Not if I molest you, it isn't."

"Are you going to molest me?" Dave asks. Then he adds, "Or are you a pathological liar!?" He scores a point, he thinks, but then Erin tugs on the thread. "Geez, ow!"

"It'll get worse before it gets better," Erin says, then she dabs the wound with hydrogen peroxide again. There are tears in Dave's eyes. He looks away from her, at the wall. "See?"

"I'm not in the mood for molestation now, I have to say."

"Give it a few minutes." For once, Erin seems to run out of things to say. But ten seconds later. "Who stabbed you?"

"I don't know. Some black kid."

"Figures," Erin says.

"Hey, that's not fair!" Dave says.

"You're the one who got stabbed," Erin says.

"Don't be racist. White people stab people too," Dave says. "And there are plenty of nice black people."

"Yeah, you're white. You ever stab anyone? Have any black friends?"

Dave almost names Lee and Malik, though he hardly knows them at all. "I've been bullied by white people too. This guy even looked half-Italian," he says.

"What does that even mean?"

"You're very ignorant."

"I'm just a stupid girl, eh?"

"Look, I didn't say that." Dave bites his lip. "Why are you picking a fight with me! All you do is needle me and upset me."

Erin tilts her head to the side. "Don't you like me? I'm just teasing you. It's a joke. Really. Listen, I'm sorry." She touches his face. Tiny little fingers on his cheek. Dave has never felt anything like that. Her eyes are glistening. "You know, I was homeschooled for a long time. We're new in town. We used to live in the city, in Astoria."

"What brought you out to Jersey City?"

Erin shrugs. "One of my second cousins owns the building, and the little luncheonette on the bottom floor. So we got this cheap. Things aren't going well at Washington Square. You know, little bratty teenagers keep walking in and then just leaving without buying anything."

"I'm sorry, I was—"

"Not even an order of fries."

"C'mon, I didn't want—"

"The McDonald's is only half a block down, sure," Erin says, "but do you know what they put in those burgers? Fifty percent hooves, thirty percent veins, twenty percent ammonia derivatives. Believe it!"

"I said I was sorry," Dave says. Even in the Ylem, where my own life is nothing but a half-remembered film, I'm riveted, because I remember what happens next. Dave blinks back a tear; he's sure he's done everything wrong. Then Erin grabs his shirt in both her little fists and pulls him in for a kiss. She's aggressive, hungry like a grown woman. She's all tongue to Dave, and he barely knows how to breathe. He keeps his hands at his sides, stunned. Finally, Erin pulls away, a thin string of drool connecting her lips to Dave's. It's the kiss I should have gotten in my own room, when she initiated me into the Ylem.

"You taste like cough syrup," she says, "and kiss like a fag," and without a word Dave dives in for a kiss, but misses her mouth and gets a face full of hair. Erin takes his arms and puts them around her waist and says, "Like this, stupid." They kiss some more. Dave can only smell cloves, and his own sweat. He wants to move his hands up and down her back, into her curls, but he's terrified.

The kisses are working—he can barely feel his suture. He wants to push forward, or lean back, but the blood is pumping everywhere. Something's going to burst. Then Erin pulls away.

"My father's coming home now. Don't ask me how I know."

"How do you know . . ." Dave says. "Uh, that I was going to ask that."

"You have to leave, right now!" Erin says. "Just out the door. You don't want him catching you in the hallway, or on the staircase. You'll really end up in the hospital if you do."

Dave opens his mouth to say something. Erin kisses his bottom lip quickly, then stands and pulls him from the bed. "Go!" she practically howls. Her fingernails dig into the flesh of his shoulder. She opens the door and pushes him out into the hallway. Dave runs, swallowing a whoop, then clutches his side and limps, leaning against the balustrade to the steps.

And there the big man is. Though Mr. Zevgolis isn't all that large. He's a squat man, and he filled up the staircase like an awkwardly shaped couch abandoned by lackadaisical movers. His eyebrows are like the wings of a great crow, and he smelled of grease even from the bottom of the stairwell.

"Who're you?"

"Uhm . . ." Dave says.

"Your shirt is bloody. You all right? How you get in here?" With every question, he climbs three steps. "You on drugs?" he says, and he's face to face with Dave. He's a short man, Mr. Zevgolis, but as wide as he is tall. A nasty scar runs down one redwood forearm. *So Erin wasn't lying about that*. Unless it was something else that cut her father so badly. The scar looks only half-healed. Dave feels his own suture burning.

"No," Dave says. "I don't know what I'm doing here."

"Maybe I call police, eh?"

"Can I go home, please?"

"Don't you never come back, you understand?" Zevgolis says. Even his teeth seem supernaturally huge, each one like a jetty.

Dave tries to squeak out an *okay* but he just exhales and bumps into Zevgolis. The man shoves past him and walks up to the near entrance of the railroad apartment. Dave runs down the steps as best he is able.

In the Journal Square neighbourhood where Erin lives, there are a number of cheap and dusty stores. The Rite Aid workers are trained to hassle kids when they want a little medicine. And they have cameras everywhere. Why Dave thinks of cameras now, he doesn't know, but it's because I was staring at him so intently from the Ylem. No cameras in 99 Cent Dreams right across the street. And they carry the Mexican cough syrup. He drinks deep as he takes the long way back home.

The police are waiting in the living room. Ann is there too, half-sober, her back straight. "David!" she cries as Dave walks in. "My baby!" She runs, as best she can, to hug him. Dave peers over her shoulder at the police—one guy in a uniform and one plainclothesman. They could be extras from *The Sopranos*, or Mr. Zevgolis's cousins. And they knew mom was faking the funk.

"The prodigal son returns," the uniformed officer says to nobody in particular. Dave squirms out of his mother's grip, and she gives it up too easily.

"They're here about a poking!" Ann stage-whispers. Dave realizes that he wishes he had a sane woman in his life. Here in the Ylem, I can see the futures branching forth from this point. There are plenty of sane women in Dave's life. They throw themselves at us in college, at the workplace, they're just an email or telephone call or kind word away, but I ignore them all to seek out this same dynamic over and over again—a woman whose modes and behaviours are beyond predicting, who are concerned with appearances, and who have some sort of wound that won't ever heal, no matter what mad actions they took to salve it. If they really like me, even for a moment, or were kind and not cutting or oblivious, I win. If I lose, well, I try and try again, across every potential future. I liked that hug, though it was as contrived as the one Dave had gotten by the cute redhead whose name we had both forgotten as part of the school play in sixth grade. He had fit in the leprechaun costume, so got the role.

The uniform murmurs something about the poking. Dave raises his shirt and shows off his homebrew suture. "It's fine," he says, unconvinced and dreamy. He coughs twice, so he'll have an explanation for the cough syrup in his book bag, for his lateness, for what he's sure are the subtle changes in his aura thanks to his first real make-out session.

"Who did that?" the detective asks.

"Uhm . . . I did it myself," Dave says.

"Not a bad job," he says, convincingly enough for Ann.

"What did the person who stabbed you look like?" the uniformed officer asks. He has a pad out.

"Black guy," Dave says. "He looked a little older, I

guess." He smiles. The cough syrup is making him feel pretty good, like he's in a theme park, chatting with costumed characters. Cop Man and the Fat Detective. They're his favourites. "He's not a student."

"What makes you think he wasn't a student?" Ann asks. "I mean, do you know every black kid in school?" She spits out the words *black kid*.

"Uhm." Dave wobbles on his feet. The uniform takes him by the shoulder and sits him down on an ottoman. "Where's dad?" he asks. "Shouldn't he be here? I'm hot. I want my dad, and a lawyer."

"You don't need a lawyer, son," the uniform says. "You're the victim here, remember?" The detective is studying the photos on the walls. There aren't many of them, none of recent vintage. Dave is ten years old in the newest, the smile flashing his last few milk teeth.

"I go to Hamilton," Dave says. "It's a bad school."

"We're not Catholic," Ann says. The cops turn to look at her. "I didn't want to send him to Catholic school. That's why he's in public school." She mutters again, "We're not Catholic."

"When is your husband due home, ma'am?" the detective asks.

"Oh, he works late," Ann says. "He's in IT, you know."

"He's in *it*!" Dave says, and giggles. Ann guffaws.

"I'm about ready to call child protective services," the detective says, and it's like a cold wind tore through the room. "Listen, ma'am, get your kid to the precinct first thing tomorrow morning, and I want a note from an ER doctor about those stitches. If I don't see him at my desk by noon, I'm going to come here and pick you up, then drive you to Hamilton and pick him up"—the detective's fat finger is seemingly pointing everywhere at once; at Ann, at Dave, at his own chest, in the direction of the school—"and then I'll bring you both back for questioning before me, a social worker, and whatever foster parents they can dig up on an hour's notice." The uniformed officer works his tongue over his teeth. Neither Ann nor Dave have the chance to say anything before they stomp out.

Finally Ann says, "I'm going to sue that cop, that wop, to atoms." She holds in a little burp, then turns to Dave, her eyes blazing. "To wop cop atoms!" she shouts. She snorts her exhalations, then her energy leaves her.

"Can we get pizza?" Dave whines. Ann doesn't answer—she's weeping softly—but Dave knows her credit card number and makes the call. He's fed himself and left the other half of the pie atop the stove to stay warmed by the pilot light, and is on his computer upstairs by the time Jeremy comes home and the shouting begins.

In the morning, Ann stays in bed. Dave wakes up to his father looming over him.

"I called the precinct. It took some doing, but you don't have to go in. Not to school and not to the police station. That asshole detective was entirely out of line," Jeremy says. There's an edge in his voice. "I made an appointment with Doctor Khan to check out your injury and your little Cub Scout first-aid attempt."

"I need to go to school," Dave says. That's where Erin will be, and Erin's ogre father won't be. "Uhm, I have a test. An important one."

"What subject?"

"Uhm, Social Studies."

"What about Social Studies?" Jeremy says.

"Well, Latin America," Dave says.

"What's the capital of Peru?"

I whisper in his ear, because I want to see Erin again too. "Lima," Dave says, a femtosecond behind me, in a version of my own voice.

"At least you studied. Fine," Jeremy says. "I have to get to work." And he leaves.

There's a war inside Dave. Erin will be in school. She should be in school anyway. But as he approaches Hamilton, he starts thinking of the guy who stabbed him. Of the little white pen the kid used. How it felt like the air was coming out of the balloon of his body. He could be anywhere in the crowds of black kids clumped by the steps. Dave manages to get himself into the building without panicking. A cough-syrup flavoured burp soothes his fevered imagination for a moment. He looks around for Erin, doesn't see her. He looks around for Oleg, doesn't see him either, and he's generally easy to spot with his ridiculous trench coat. Dave can't bring himself to walk down the hallway where it happened, but homeroom is at the end of that hall. He can't do it. His feet won't move. The guy with the pen could be anywhere, behind any door, ready with his Bic. Finally, Dave heads up to the school's third floor, walks across the parallel hallway, takes the steps back down to the other end of the hallway on the second floor, then makes it to homeroom just as the door opens and the kids pour out. *Oh, Mr. Holbrook*, he thinks, *it's going to be a day.* And then a hand like a canned ham clamps down on his shoulder and his knees quake and he waits for the next burst of pain, but it's only the detective.

"I told your father you didn't have to come in. But I

didn't tell him that I was going to leave you alone," he says. Officer Levine is behind him, looking like a scolded child. "We got an appointment in the principal's office." Dave wonders why the detective didn't introduce himself, didn't even give a name. He doesn't find out till he arrives at the principal's office, and one of the secretaries says, "Detective Giovanni, Doctor Furgeson will see you now."

"Of course he will," Giovanni snorts. To Dave he nods toward the door leading to the interior office and says, "Walk."

"Mr. Holbrook," Doctor Furgeson says. "Thank you for coming." Doctor Furgeson is the principal. He's a tiny fellow—wiry with red hair turning quickly grey, and pale freckles. Until now, Dave always imagined him sitting on Mr. Fusco's shoulders as the big vice principal strode down the halls of the school, calling out orders and making demands.

"The police took me here. I was late to homeroom. I don't want today on my record as a cut," Dave says.

"Yes, the stabbing was a terrible thing. You're very brave. Is that what the perpetrator said?" Furgeson asks. He attempts a comical "black" accent and says, "'I cut yo ass!'" This voice sounds like a squeaky door. Dave looks over at Officer Levine, whose eyes are wide and trembling.

"Shouldn't my mom be here?" Dave asks. Giovanni laughs a single loud *ha!* at that.

"We need to get to the bottom of this, Mr. Holbrook. So you told the police that the perpetrator wasn't a student?" Dave opens his mouth to answer, but the principal just continues speaking. "I find this difficult to believe. We check IDs and have metal detectors at every entrance, you see?"

"I was attacked with a pen!" Dave says.

"There's metal in pens." The principal looks at the detective as he speaks. "So I wonder if Mr. Holbrook isn't trying to actually protect his assailant, for fear of reprisals."

"The metal detector would go off constantly if pens set it off. We're in a school."

"Do you have a lot of gang violence in Hamilton?"

"I'd say gang affiliations more than violence," Officer Levine says.

"It's like that show *Oz* in here," Dave says. "It's like South Africa. Everything's so racial." He's saying anything that comes to mind now, just to get someone to acknowledge his existence. "I have a feeling the school encourages all this, to keep us at one another's throats. There has to be someone gaining from all this. Follow the money! Isn't that the rule—follow the money?"

"Half the school is Latino," Office Levine explains to the detective. "If there was really any gang problem, there wouldn't be any gang problem for long. One faction would dominate."

"Perhaps we can make a move toward requiring school uniforms," Doctor Furgeson says.

"Is that even legal?" Levine says. The detective remains silent, taking it all in. Then he says, "There could be internecine struggles between different elements of the Hispanic community. Puerto Ricans versus Dominicans, for example."

"Why do all the black kids sit together in the

cafeteria?" Furgeson wonders aloud. "Speaking of . . . are we ready, Mr. Levine?"

Officer Levine gets on his walkie-talkie and asks someone on the other end if everything is ready to go. The detective checks his watch. Dave wants to ask what internecine means—he underestimated the detective. SAT words. They then all leave the office, Dave following like a mere victim of gravity. Oleg is waiting in the exterior office. He waves. A few other kids are waiting too. All white, and all, to be blunt, nerds. Hamilton is a big school, so Dave doesn't know them all, but he can tell. Awkward glasses, greasy hair, elbows and knees everywhere. Underdeveloped weirdos with last year's book bag and clothes selected by aping what Peter Parker was wearing two decades ago in the comics.

"Have all of you been stabbed too?" Dave asks. "Oleg?"

"What? No," Oleg says. Nobody else answers. They've likely never been to the principal's office before, and are just as confused as Dave. They're marched out of the office as a group, with the principal leading the way and Levine behind. Detective Giovanni hangs off to the side, like he's worried about germs. They're led through the halls, to the annex and the cafeteria. It's surprisingly full and quiet, for 9:30 in the morning, but Dave and the nerds figure it out quickly. Everyone seated is black, and a boy, and burning with a sullen resentment. Several other police officers are in the cafeteria as well, stationed in pairs by the exits. Dave and the others are herded through the space, threading through the aisles. The kids are mostly quiet, but Lee smiles and waves at Dave and says, "Yo!" All the boys at the table glare, and Malik, who is sitting right next to him, rolls his eyes and snorts.

"No talking," Officer Levine tells Dave. Everyone knows he meant Dave. Then the small troupe marches back out the far entrance of the cafeteria and is brought into the nearby boy's locker room, adjacent to the gymnasium.

"Thank you, fellows," Doctor Furgeson says. "You may all go."

"But . . ." one of the smaller kids whines, "we need hall passes. We'll get in trouble."

"Just go," the detective says. There's a burst of collective yawps and talking, but the detective puts his fingers to his lips. The boys shut up and leave, except for Dave, and Oleg, who takes a few steps away, but loiters nearby.

"Mr. Broukian?" Doctor Furgeson says.

"I want to know what's going on," Oleg says. "Dave'll tell me afterwards anyway, so I may as well stay and hear now."

"Tigger, it's okay—"

"Tigger?" Furgeson interrupts. "Is that some kind of nickname?"

"What else would it be?" Oleg says.

"Mr. Fusco told me it had some special significance. Is it a gang nickname?"

"Yeah," Oleg says, "it's a gang nickname. Pooh Corner, represent." Dave laughs at that, and so does Officer Levine. The principal tells the police officer to escort Oleg back to class. "Call me, Davey!" Oleg says as he marches out, raising his feet high in a hint of a goosestep.

"So," Giovanni says. "You recognize your assailant in there?"

"In the cafeteria? No. Did you bring all the black guys

into the cafeteria for me to check out, like a line-up?"

"I didn't do a thing," the detective says.

"Mr. Holbrook, David," Doctor Furgeson says. "It's just not possible that you were stabbed by a non-student. Do you understand? It had to have been a student. Our security is too tight."

"Is it even legal, what you did?" Dave asks. He looks at the detective, who pretends not to hear the question. "You know, if we all keep asking if things are legal, that probably means illegal things are happening."

"Does your mother drink a lot, son?" Giovanni asks. "Do you? Speaking of legal."

"Now, you said it was an African-American male, your assailant—" Furgeson says.

"Well, I don't see what that has to do with anything."

"Maybe you drink a little too," the detective says.

"Please don't try to make this a racial issue. We took care to make sure you couldn't be easily identified. That's why we had you walk through the cafeteria with those other boys. Now, stop trying to protect a criminal and—"

"I've got a theory," the detective says. "You stabbed yourself. Maybe it was an accident. Maybe you were embarrassed."

"Mr. Fusco says that Oleg Broukian was with you. Did he do it?" Furgeson says. "Is that why he was so eager to stick around?"

Dave takes a seat on the long bench between lockers. "This is all insane. I want to talk to my parents."

"Problems at home? I talked to your father before. He was—"

"Mr. Holbrook, I'll be pleased to call your parents,"

says Furgeson. "We can all go together back into the cafeteria and you can identify your assailant with their help, perhaps."

Call them. Call them right now. And they'll call the news, and you can explain why you brought all those black kids into the cafeteria. That's what I wanted to say. What I willed Dave to say over and over, through countless iterations of this morning. Instead, all he said was a weak little, "Don't."

"Don't interrupt me again," the detective tells Furgeson. "Your father thinks he's a little tough guy," he says to Dave. "If he's so tough, why is his kid such a mess, and his wife, oh man . . ." He shakes his head.

There's a reason I loved Erin, despite everything. There's no need for suspense—there can be no such thing in the Ylem anyway—she hired the man who stabbed Dave. He went to the community college near her apartment, ate at the luncheonette on the ground floor. Sometimes he worked at her father's diner. Dave was easy enough to describe, and she wouldn't have cared had he stabbed a few other geeky guys with a pen and then ran. She even helped him sneak into the school, and paid him off with her mouth. But now, as Dave squirmed on that little bench, she did something wonderful. She pulled a fire alarm.

"That's not a drill," Furgeson says as it echoes throughout the locker room.

"It's a false alarm," the detective says.

"Doesn't matter, we have to get outside. I need to be out front in forty-five seconds. There are no false alarms." Furgeson grins wide. The power dynamic has shifted a little bit, even if his advantage is based on state regulations instead of native intelligence, fists the size of gallon milk jugs, and a gun.

"That Tigger kid pulled the alarm to help his little buddy out," the detective says, but Furgeson is gone, and Dave sees his chance too and runs out after the principal.

The halls are already full of once-mousy teachers all barking as they march backward with obedient students swarming after them. Furgeson charges ahead, so Dave just attaches himself to the end of some class of seniors. The alarm drowns out most of the conversations, but Dave can't help but hear his nickname once or twice as he is led outside. *White fag. There's that white faggot. Fucking punk-ass faggot.*

News travels fast. Plenty of people had heard that he was the particular white fucking faggot who got stabbed. *How's he still walkin'?* someone asks. *When I stab a motherfucker, they stay stabbed*, someone else—a girl, that time—declares. Furgeson's bizarre show in the cafeteria was a flop. Everyone knew why they'd been dragged down there: the black kids so that one of them could be identified by the white faggot, and the other white faggots as decoys. Dave was tempted to run home, to forget school entirely and forever. Do a GED in a couple of years, maybe get some homeschooling online, forge his mother's signature. Whatever it takes to get out of here. He wouldn't even need to run, he could just take a pen from his bag, work it under the suture, tear open the thread, and bleed till they send him home, or to the emergency room again.

The police from the cafeteria cordon off the street, and the student body floods into it. Furgeson gets his hands on a megaphone and announces that if the alarm was a false one, whoever pulled it was going to be "Suspended, expelled, arrested, tried, and convicted. And also fined," he adds as an afterthought. Then, somewhere on the far side of Newark Avenue, a fight breaks out. Dave didn't care to see it, but is pushed forward as the crowd runs to check out the ruckus. It's everyone's favourite: a girl-fight. Dave doesn't know either of the girls—both Latinas, one chunky, the other wire-thin and tall and dark, going at it, shrieking in two languages, thrashing in the grips of their boyfriends, and then the cops, aiming for the eyes. The tall one is pulled right off the asphalt, and just kicks the chubby girl in the head. Her head snaps back, but she's not done. She bursts the hold the cop has on her and plows into the tall girl and the two police holding her. Then the rest of the cops pile atop them, grabbing ankles and wrists.

Time to go, Mr. Holbrook, Dave thinks, and he takes the opportunity to squeeze into the dead spaces between clumps of students to get onto Pavonia Avenue. He has the idea to just head into the city. The PATH train is only a buck, one way. He could make a day of it. Every decision is a universe unto itself, and in a dynamic group there were many decisions—turn left or right, duck down or rise up to the balls of one's feet, stay still or run for it— that every kid filling the street outside the school could make. And here comes a fire truck, despite the absence of fire, or even smoke. There's a world where I stayed put, paralyzed by anxiety and curiosity, and then just shuffled back into the school building like everyone else. One where I ran for it, made it to Manhattan, and stayed there for four cold nights before going home; and one where I made it to Manhattan and stayed there for three years, living in a squat till my blood grew poisoned and I died. One where I just went home and stayed truant for three days till my father threatened to call the police.

But this world—the one I'm watching now—is the one where Dave turns and runs, and walks right into a waiting fist. Dave doesn't know who the guy is, but he had been in the cafeteria, and had sussed Dave out as the catalyst for his ruined morning. The bone that makes up his eye socket crunches hard, and his face and eyes fill with blood. The crowd hoots and *ooohs*. He doesn't even fall to the ground before his assailant grabs a fistful of windbreaker, picks him back up and punches him again on the side of the head. That first blow was a miracle of brutality, but the next few don't do much. Dave already has a broken nose, after all. He's unconscious and hard to actually hold up with one hand. It's like smacking around a rag doll, except that this one is built to bruise. Dave's eyes flicker open and he thinks he sees something. Huge black wings. Oleg and his trench coat, on the back of the attacker, trying some goofy wrestling hold. Oleg gets shrugged off. He throws two ineffectual punches at the big kid's back. There's laughter everywhere. Someone else—Erin obviously, though Dave can't tell Erin from a telephone pole at the moment—grabs Dave by the shoulders and leads him away to sit on the curb. Oleg hits the asphalt hard, and then the cops swoop in, truncheons in hand. More sirens—police this time, not fire trucks.

"Not bad, eh?" Erin says to Dave.

Dave opens his mouth to talk but Erin holds up a hand. "Don't talk. Keep working on your breathing. And don't blow the blood out of your nose; your eyes will swell shut. With a fire truck comes an ambulance, always, so just hang on, okay?"

Dave nods.

"You know, they say high school is the best time of our lives, and that we should do all we can to enjoy these carefree days before entering the real world. I have to agree. What a sunny day. It's great to be outside instead of trapped in those stuffy old classrooms," she says. "It's like I can smell the asbestos. Good thing there was a real fire, eh?"

Dave says, "Whus goin' on? Why?" He raises his arms, trying to encompass the whole scene before them. A dozen cop cars have arrived. The businesses along the street are closing early, pulling metal gratings down over their display windows. A helicopter hovers right over the school. The soap operas and morning news programs have been pre-empted for the live media feed. Somehow, Dave and Erin are invisible in the midst of the discord.

"You know, you're totally going to wake up in the hospital," Erin says. "I wonder how your folks will deal with it. Think they'll finally pull you out of this shithole school?"

Dave shakes his head. "Mah duh wond . . ."

"Don't speak, don't speak," Erin says, a finger on his lips. "You sound like a retard." She takes his hand and puts it on her chest. "There. This is a first for you, isn't it?" Dave swoons, and falls to the curb.

CHAPTER 12

Prison is a lot like high school. By that I mean that every motherfucker here deserves a fucking bullet in their head, with their mamas watching on TV as it happens. I'm famous enough that I have a cell to myself; it's full of books and presents, and I even have my own computer. I'm like Mumia Abu-Jamal in here. French fucking novelists visit me, and their interviews with me appear in prestigious Communist literary journals. This is the life. Shooting up Hamilton really did solve all my problems.

Like I was telling one of those French fags the other day on Skype, "It's all about carving out a little bit of free will. Aren't all of you people supposed to be beret-wearing existentialists? You should know that you're free all the time, but afraid of it. Well, something happened to me and then I wasn't afraid anymore." Sadly for the world, the art of the follow-up question has been lost, so he didn't ask me what happened. What turned me from Dave into I, into the Kallis Episkopos! What made it so easy for me to pick up a machine gun and, with no experience in shooting at all, paint the hallways red.

I credit my existential cosmic freedom to cough syrup. I feel sorry for the youth of today. When I was in high school, you could walk into any drugstore and buy the stuff with little grief. Now they want to see ID, they keep records, take photos. I'm not even talking about the sizzurp—the prescription stuff—I mean plain old over-the-counter meds sufficient for a little robotrippin'.

I used to use a lot. It changes your perceptions. I understood things other people couldn't. I knew that the goddess of discord, Eris herself, was a student at Hamilton, and she was attempting to manipulate events to create a bloodbath. Why New Jersey? Why the twenty-first century? Let's just say that there's always a bloodbath going on somewhere, and it's hardly beyond the ability of a goddess to be in more than one place at a time.

And I saw something else. I saw myself, sitting atop the world, where the ice caps meet the sky, in a throne made of glacial ice. And due to my body heat, the ice began to melt and the trickling slush formed a thousand rivers and a million tributaries. And my face was reflected in the tiny chunks and particles of ice. Every little stream was a life of mine. The great big me atop the throne could see them all at once, and frown, or shake his head, or smile at his endless mistakes. But I, the me in my little purple drank haze, had to do it the hard way. Follow every stream to its end. Killed by the police. Dead in the incubator at three weeks old from a lung infection. Bad tin of sardines at age thirty-one. Or me, shooting my way through school and surrendering to the police. It's a scandal. *Things* are blamed: video games, the Internet, lax morality, my supposed homosexuality, drunk mother, distant father, and, of course, race. I get poorly written fan letters from the chinless daughters of white supremacist Pineys to this day. I saw it all coming. I chose the path, chose to be manipulated by Eris, and have set myself up in the best of all possible worlds. A world that stretches before me, into infinity.

I tried to tell this all to my shrink, a few times. I knew she'd refuse to engage me—can't feed into a patient's delusions by taking them seriously enough to challenge, after all. But I also knew she'd finally cave in.

"Fine, then," she said. "You know, already, everything about your life."

"I do."

"As though you are someone else, observing yourself from the outside. Watching a video of your own life, from beginning to end, and you can rewind, or freeze frame—"

"And listen to, and record my own director's commentary as a special feature!"

"But you cannot change your fate. Dave Holbrook is just the main character in the video. Is that correct?"

"More or less. I mean, I decided which DVD of *I* to watch. And live."

"So then, you must have at least skipped to the end of all of them in order to choose which life was most satisfying."

"That's right."

She raised her palms to the cracked ceiling and gestured around us. "And this is the one you chose."

"That's also right."

"So then, how does Dave Holbrook die?"

I just stared at her. She rolled her eyes. I suppose that the superior breed of psychologists end up working in places a little tonier than East Jersey State Prison. "How does *I* die?" she asked.

"How do I die? Or how do you die?" I laughed at my own little joke. It gets funnier every time I tell it to her. She raised her right hand and pointed her finger at me like it was a gun. I lifted my own finger and drew my symbol—three toothy little peaks and valleys—in response.

"Resistance. Electricity. Everything moving very quickly, as if superheated, and then it all stops at once."

"You're not on death row, Da—I. New Jersey eliminated the death penalty five years ago. There's no electric chair in your future. Old Smokey is a museum piece."

"Just try to act surprised when it happens, all right?"

"Our time is over for now, Mr. Holbrook."

O

Ironically, there's something very freeing about knowing one's own fate. Some Spic tried to shank me the other day, but I knew it wasn't going to work. The hacks had been tipped off—by me, having forged a note from one of their preferred drug customers—and they tackled the guy and broke his arm while I sat in the common area, playing countertop football with a bit of folded paper against my friend the retarded sex offender. I wasn't able to act surprised, but that just adds to my mystique. In my vision, there was a web of tributaries branching off the stream of my prison sentence. In some I'm punked so hard and so often I go fag and prance around in lipstick and bleach-blonde hair. In others, I don't make it that far—choked out and left to die in solitary by a hack whose cousin had gone to Hamilton but never graduated thanks to me. But in this particular babbling brook I'm wading through, nothing goes wrong until the end. I never get to see the outside again, or take a bus, or see her, but life is good. Conjugal visits from groupies with too much eye makeup. The occasional sit-down interview with a crusading journalist—I give them a three-star looney-toon act as requested—and a law library with which to amuse myself. My life is better than my shrink's life, that's for sure. It's good. It'll be a good, long life.

CHAPTER 13

Dave wakes up in the hospital. This is the awakening he remembers. First he spat out some gibberish to the EMTs on the trip to St. Mary's Hospital in Hoboken. He tries to walk out of the ER and into the parking lot while being triaged. When he wakes up for the third time, he stays conscious and remembers. Dave's entire face feels the way a 3D movie looks—like it's floating in front of him in exactly the wrong spot. Only slowly does he become aware of the wider world. His mother Ann sitting next to him, sober but practically sweating alcohol. The curtains on either side of the bed—Dave is not in a room, nor is he in a ward. The noise and bustle beyond the curtains. He senses something else nearby too—it's me—but only for a moment, then he is no longer able to experience me as I experience him.

"Mom?" Dave asks. Tears blind him.

"Oh honey," Ann says. "I'm so sorry. Daddy is meeting with a lawyer now. We're suing the school, we're suing the district, the state of New Jersey—it controls the schools, after all. And we'll find someplace for you. Someplace without riots and stabbings and nonsense. Don't fall asleep; the doctors think you might have a concussion, and with your nose already messed up . . ."

It was the nicest thing my mother had ever said, in this timeline or any other. She was beyond "up" and "down"—she was actually a mother for once. If Erin hadn't pulled the fire alarm, Dave never would have been spotted and punched in the face so ferociously and so publicly. If she hadn't been there to sit him down on the curb, he would have been beaten down that much harder. Ann would have been drunk beyond kindness by the time Dave regained consciousness. Instead, she would have hissed, *What the hell did you do to bring this upon yourself!* and shriek her demand for an answer until a pair of orderlies dragged her outside.

But Dave only has a mind for Erin, who helped him to the curb and held his hand. "But . . . school," he says, as best he is able.

"Sshh." Ann puts her fingers to her own lips, then to those of her son. "Just rest now. Your father is on his way. He had to leave work early to come, so don't agitate him with talk of wanting to stay in that horrible zoo." She licks her lips and wrings her hands to hide the shakes. Then the kindness is gone, replaced by an urgent need. "Listen, Davey," his mother says, "I'll be right back. I have to find the restroom." Dave is alone. He wants the restroom too, but can't manage to get up, and he's too embarrassed to use the bedpan, so he waits and squirms.

Ann doesn't come back, but Jeremy finally does. His face tells Dave the story—the kid is a problem to be solved. "Where's your mother?" he starts, but then immediately changes topics. "How are you feeling? Are you in a lot of pain? Do you need a painkiller?" And without waiting for an answer he says, "Let me get a nurse," and then pushes his way through the curtains and bellows for a nurse. One comes soon enough, and happily hands Dave some pills, which he just as happily takes, but all he really wants is some Robitussin. *Maybe later*, he thinks, *once my parents are gone*.

Jeremy badgers the nurse. When will he get a room? A private or a semi-private? There were other kids injured today; how can he be guaranteed that his son won't be put in the same room as one of those animals? How much is this going to cost? What did those pills cost? Fifty bucks a piece or something? And to each question the nurse only says, "I don't know, sir," with the *s* in *sir* growing ever more sibilant. Finally, she says she has other patients to attend to and leaves.

Jeremy takes the seat his wife had vacated and sighs. "Would more Tae Kwon Do lessons help, you think?"

"Dad . . . the whole school. Police . . ."

"Well, what the hell are we supposed to do? Buy you a gun?" He runs his hand over his face as if trying to wipe off his features. "Sorry, son. This is just so frustrating. There's no standard operating procedure for this sort of event. I can imagine that your mother has one. It's the same as it is for anything else." He pantomimed drinking from a flask. "I'll talk to her about it after this all blows over. This has to end now, David."

"What am I supposed to do?" The pain is fading, but the opiates haven't yet taken hold. Dave's alert now and upset, unused to having extended conversations with his father about anything.

"Maybe we'll move. Sell the house. Prices are skyrocketing. I can find a place closer to work. New school, new everything. But you need to do your part. How many scrapes are you going to get into; how much trouble is there going to be? You have to be doing something to make yourself a target. There are two thousand kids in that school, and they're not *all* coming home looking that they went twelve rounds with Mike Tyson. If you spent less time on that damn computer and more time making some friends, you wouldn't be such a target." Jeremy sighs again, and slaps his palms against his thighs. "I wasn't like you in school. I had friends, a girlfriend, excellent grades. Did you know I was three-year varsity on the golf team?"

"We don't even have a golf team. Where the hell would we practice!? This isn't Long Island, you know," Dave says. It hurts to talk so much, so angrily. He knows his father will focus on the word *hell*, and of course Jeremy does.

"Don't talk to me that way," Jeremy says. "Respect at all times. *Respect!* You know that the specific example of the golf team isn't the point. You haven't gone out for anything. Hell, the chess club would be an improvement. Glee club. Towel manager!"

"Now you're the one saying hell. And—"

"Father," Jeremy says, pointing to himself. "Child." He points to Dave. "That's the difference, and it's a *hell* of a difference."

"And anyway, we don't have a chess club or a glee club or towel—"

"Oh no, now that's a lie! I'm sure you have towel managers, because Hamilton has a football team. And a basketball team. Oh boy, don't try to tell me there isn't a basketball team at Hamilton," Jeremy says, voice thick and nasty. "You need to get it together, son. I want to hear a plan from you by the end of the week. Something to improve your situation. Understand?"

"Yes, Dad."

"Good," Jeremy says. He slides his Blackberry from his pocket and thumbs the keys for a moment. "I have to go. And, uh, find your mother. They'll probably let you out tomorrow; I'll be here to pick you up, son. Don't use or consume anything you don't have to. Even paper slippers are fourteen dollars, apparently. God knows what'll happen if you eat a bowl of apple sauce. I bet that's not covered by insurance." He stands and, without another word or even a backward glance, pulls the curtain, walks through, and shuts it behind him.

"What an asshole." Dave thinks that, but it's Erin who says it, from Dave's left, behind the other curtain. She pops her head in and smiles. Erin's smile is always squinty, but it's warped now because her left eye is sporting a serious shiner. She's not in her casual school clothes either, but a candy striper outfit. "What do you think?" she says, running her hands down her sides.

"Uhm . . . do you really work here?"

"I started today."

"When you found that outfit hanging up somewhere, right?"

Erin nods. "You're pretty smart, eh?"

"Why do you do these crazy things? It's just nuts. Someone's going to get in trouble," Dave says.

"Oleg found me in the hallway while you were being worked over in the locker room. He told me what happened. I pulled the fire alarm. I guess that caused all the fights, eh?" Erin says. She takes a step closer to the bed.

"I guess . . . wait, I wasn't being 'worked over.'"

"No? Too bad, it sounded sexy." She puts her hand on his knee, over the thin cloth sheet. "Say, can I get you anything. Some water? A book? A magazine? Maybe *Penthouse Forum*?" Her palm brushes across his crotch.

"Oh God, stop," Dave says. "I don't feel good. How come we didn't do this before . . . I can barely breathe." And he can barely breathe. He starts gasping, gagging. He smacks Erin away and grabs the call button. "I'll call, stop!"

Erin pulls back. "Fine! I'll find someone who really likes me. Somewhere else. And it'll definitely be easy. I'm not going to waste any more time with a baby like you." She storms out. Dave thinks it's so strange that the curtains have pretty much managed to keep people out. The whole afternoon was like a little play, with one person entering and then leaving, one after the other. But now the play is over and he is alone, without even a television to entertain him. He turns the call button over in his hand, but realizes he has no requests for the nurse. What's he going to do, ask for a hug? He closes his eyes and cries, then sleeps.

Dave wakes up in another room. It must be at least two in the morning, or that's his guess. Someone else, an old man, is in the room on the other side of the curtain. He's on the second floor now, his bed by the window. The parking lot is nearly empty of cars, and there is plenty of light thanks to an emergency pavilion. A woman walks into view. She's small. Could be anybody, but Dave thinks it's Erin. Or his mother. They're roughly the same size and shape. She stops right beyond the pool of light, almost purposefully to remain a silhouette, then raises one hand high. Then she snaps it down, as if pulling a great invisible switch.

CHAPTER 14

My job has benefits. I don't mean the pretty nice benefits of a state employee, but particular benefits. The state lottery is a part of the New Jersey State Department of the Treasury, and that's what my work ID reads, what my business cards read, and what the voicemail on my work phone explains to callers. Theoretically, I could even get a license to carry a gun with relative ease, except for my high school escapade.

My job's not a bad one. One would think that there wouldn't be much call for lottery machine installations—doesn't every ugly little bodega and liquor store have one already? Well, the stores close and then open again under new management some months later. New ones open up. Machines break or even get ripped off by the special sort of idiot who thinks having a machine means being able to make it cough up winning numbers in advance. So most days I work in the field, which I prefer to the warehouse or my cubicle. I love driving, even in New Jersey.

Most days I don't run into anyone I know. There

was that guy Charles from high school, once, and very occasionally someone recognizes me from the newspaper stories, but that's only when I'm working in Jersey City. Today, I ran into someone else—Mr. McCann, my old Social Studies teacher. I was working in a new liquor store in Harrison. Harrison's an odd little town carved out in a small jetty of land by Newark. I lived in North Jersey all my life, but never had occasion to visit there, knew nobody who worked or lived here, and only knew about it at all because it has a PATH station stop of its own. I've never even felt the need to get out and walk around to see what's what. But there I was, driving the lottery van down 3rd Street, looking for the cleverly named 3rd Street Liquors, when McCann stormed across the street. I had to slam on my brakes. He whipped his head around to look at me. It was him. Older and grey, both his hair and his skin, I mean, and he was unshaven. His eyes were wild; he would have killed me if he could. But he couldn't. His lips quivered for a moment, and then he ran to the sidewalk and into the store. Into 3rd Street Liquors, the very store I'd been looking for.

It's easy to park when driving an official vehicle, so I parked right in front of the place. It was 10:15 a.m. I had no choice but to go about my business. McCann wasn't going to come out if I was outside, and he probably didn't know that I was heading into the liquor store myself. He was the one who had saved my life, and the lives of a lot of other students. After what happened between Erin and my father—between *Eris* and my father, I should say—and the endless insults and injuries of school, I thought I'd put the fear of God into everyone at Hamilton. I had no plans to shoot anyone, and I didn't shoot anyone. I was just going to wave a gun around, scare some people. I figured that if I had a reputation for being "crazy" people would leave me alone, or I'd at least be thrown out of school.

McCann cared about me about as much as anyone in that school did—not at all. But he had cultivated the bad habit of coming in early and smoking a cigarette while eating his McDonald's breakfast on the corner about a block from the school. We passed one another on the street that day. I didn't say hello; in Jersey, you don't say "hi" to acquaintances you encounter outside. You might nod and raise your eyebrows. Teachers you ignore. The courtesy is supposed to be mutual, but that day McCann spotted me and decided to follow me. I was wearing Oleg's long leather duster, which set him off. I'd told Oleg I needed the trench coat to hide my kilt, which I was planning on wearing to protest the proposed dress code at the assembly this afternoon. Oleg was always in favour of anything weird and stupid. But it was only three years after Columbine, and a picked-on kid strolling purposefully toward high school was enough for McCann. In those days, cell phones weren't all that common among schoolteachers and other people who made no friggin' money, so all he could do was tail me and hope to somehow intervene.

"Mr. Holbrook!" he had shouted at me. For a second, I thought it was my imagination, but then I realized that McCann was behind me. I ran up the steps, toward the entrance nearer the INDUSTRY sign. There was a metal detector there, of course, but nobody as yet manning it, and the doors were open. That's Jersey City for you. I ran in, and in the foyer a fat guard, who had squeezed himself into one of our little plastic classroom desk chairs, looked up from his own breakfast of a bagel and grape soda, then looked back down at it when he saw it was me. What the hell was I going to do? Bring in a gun and shoot everybody? The stupid metal detector wasn't even plugged in.

"Mr. Holbrook!" I wasn't in shape, and I had a machine gun under my coat, but McCann was old, and a smoker, and only half-committed to confronting me, so I tore far ahead of him, down the hall and into . . . where? I had no plan, no place to go. Homeroom was locked, and I could hardly go through my day normally with the coat on the entire time. If I went to my hiding place, and my second gun, there was no guarantee I wouldn't be spotted and my bolthole discovered. At Hamilton, about ten percent of the student body came to school just to aimlessly wander the halls before lunch. Then they'd retire to the curb to smoke cigarettes and listen to music and shout at the passing cars.

So I turned around and looked at Mr. McCann, his face ruddy like an Irish drunk. "What?"

"Uhm . . ." Now he didn't know what to say. Ask me to open my coat and if I had a gun, then what? Ask me to open my coat and if I didn't have a gun, well that's a sexual harassment suit waiting to happen, now isn't it? "You're here early today."

"Yes," I'd said.

"Well then, I'll put you to some use. I have something to pick up at the principal's office, and need an extra pair of hands." He wheezed as he spoke. McCann was smart. I couldn't rightly refuse without him getting even more suspicious, and the principal's office would necessarily trump any dumbass excuse I could think of. So I pulled the gun.

McCann threw up his hands and shouted, "Don't shoot!" He was half-panicked but still thinking. The security guard extracted himself from his chair and started trotting toward us.

"Get down," I said. "Get down and nobody will get hurt." McCann got down, but didn't take his eyes from me. The security guard caught sight of the gun just as McCann lowered himself to the floor. Minimum wage wasn't worth it, I suppose, because he just screamed, "Holy shit!" and ran. I ran after him and shouted, "You touch your walkie-talkie, you die!" He kept his hands high and pumping. Behind me, I heard McCann clamber to his feet and run. I ran out of the school and got three blocks before the cop cars found me.

Someone was banging on the window of the car. "Mistah!" a guy was shouting at me. He was South Asian, angry, and probably the owner of the liquor store. "You okay? Do you have the machine?" I wasn't, but I did. I wanted to ask him if McCann was still in the store, but didn't. Part of me wanted the confrontation. After my gun was impounded and my mother came to get me, after the psychologists and journalists and the evening news, McCann quit. I never saw him again. Part of me wanted to.

The liquor store was bustling. I've long stopped being surprised by anything I see while on the job. The owner had cleared a space for me on the counter and I got to work. Like most liquor stores, this one had security mirrors hung in strategic locations, and I was able to keep track of McCann from three different angles. It was a strange experience. Usually, I'm so worried about what people think of me. The people in that Jersey City bodega, stupid Mindy from across the street, guys in the office, my shrieking mother who never lets me forget anything from her labour pains to her bailing me out of prison to my dead father—you name it. I constantly talk to myself, recite my life story as it happens, because I need to figure out what people think of me, what impact I have on them. But I didn't care what McCann thought of me. I just liked that he clearly was thinking of me, after all these years. Did I ruin his life like I supposedly ruined my parents' lives, and like I had certainly ruined my own? Is that why he's a before-noon drunk in Harrison?

I ran the machine through its testing procedures, had the owner retest it, and then had him sign off. As I was leaving, I heard that voice again: "Mr. Holbrook!" It was McCann, older and wilted.

"That's me," I said. McCann was holding a small bottle of Slivovitz, and a handful of beef jerky strips. The classic signs of a human wreck. He didn't even think to grab something classier to show off in front of me, or to wait till after I left to do his morning groceries.

But I was wrong again. "It's good to see you," he said. "You seem . . . all right, eh? I was worried about you. So worried . . ."

"Well yes, everything's fine," I said. I could have apologized to him, but I just didn't want to. My father always made me apologize for the endless imagined slights my mother complained about, and the words always stuck in my throat. I liked this encounter after all. I shouldn't have waited outside on the curb. "Should I have been worried about you?" The rhetorical knife felt good in my hand.

"Yes, of course you should have," McCann said. His teacherly timbre returned to his voice for a moment. "And you also should have been concerned about yourself. You were very lucky that the police didn't shoot you, that you weren't arrested and sent to an adult prison. Do you have any idea what they would have done to the likes of you?" His hands shook and the plastic wrap of his beef jerky crinkled loudly in his grip. Then he said it, *sotto voce*. "Faggot." McCann kept whispering, an edge in his voice. "Just because you're a faggot you think you can get away with ruining people's lives, their careers? Fucking fags like you ruin it for the rest of us!"

"The rest of us!" I laughed. "Are you coming out of the closet to me?"

"Oh yeah, you'd like that," McCann says. "You can suck my cock right here, just like a little tenth grader who wants a better grade." He lifted his right arm, making to throw his booze at me.

I put up my hands. "Take it easy, old man." He didn't throw the bottle, but he took another step toward me, so I went to the car and opened the trunk. I was fast, he was slow. I pulled out the state-regulation tire iron and slapped it against my palm. "I'm not a kid anymore. I don't have to eat a bowl of shit whenever someone offers it up to me. If you want to go, you'll be going . . . to the hospital." It wasn't a great threat, but I hadn't been in a situation like this since high school. I never had to try to intimidate someone who was actually smaller and weaker than me. But I still needed the weapon. Then we both heard the thick *ka-chunk* of a shotgun being readied. The liquor store cashier was staring at us from the doorway with his arms crossed over his chest. Behind him, a giant stockboy fresh from the pages of a Steinbeck novel had a shotgun in his hands.

"Take it elsewhere . . . boys," the cashier said.

"You're not going to shoot us in broad daylight," McCann said, still angry.

"No, but if you're not out of here in three seconds, I'm banning you from the store for life," the cashier said. And then he looked at me. "And I'll call my alderman, and the *Star-Ledger*, and some guy I know down in Trenton and I'll guarantee you won't be able to get work catching rats in Camden." That took the wind out of McCann, and there was no percentage in me waiting around anymore. With my luck, some do-gooder with a cellphone camera would be along to snap a picture of me and my state-issued tire iron. Without a word, I walked around the car to the driver's side, got in, put the tire iron on my lap, and left.

In the Ylem, I realized something—that poor schmuck hadn't had a pleasant conversation involving more than one other person in years. Fast-food restaurant servers, our mother Ann, one co-worker or supervisor at a time, the occasional odd phone call to a Match.com woman—that was Dave Holbrook's life. Group interactions necessarily meant animosity, ridicule, and occasionally the threat of violence. I whispered this in his ear, playing the role of introspection, but I was deaf to myself, as I knew he would be. I saw his life all the way to the end already, after all. An accident with a belt in a closet. My awareness extends only until the moment of death, and there's no alternative where I try that sort of erotic stunt and survive, so I have no idea what happens next. Does Ann find the body immediately, or does it take a few days for it to get ripe, like strange fruit, and finally rouse her from the couch? Does she shriek in fear and pain, or lash out angrily at the corpse, berating and belittling it, though of course even I can't hear her, and nobody can answer her. I wouldn't put it past my old mother to yell at her son's dead body. She always took everything so personally. In the Ylem I rarely laugh, as laughter requires surprise and surprise requires a limitation of information and awareness. But I imagine my mother looking at my dead body, limbs puffy and blue, and shouting at me, "You did this on purpose to ruin my Thursday! You do this all the time!" and my guffaw echoes across the endless plane of my existence.

CHAPTER 15

Dave is out of the hospital the next morning. That is to say, he is discharged. As a dependent minor he's not allowed to leave without the company of a parent or guardian, but neither Jeremy nor Ann has made an appearance. I know that Jeremy made Ann swear that she would pick up their son, and she promptly forgot, having grown distracted with white wine and some home makeover TV show. Jeremy knew she might; he was mostly interested in extracting the promise and adding it to his store of grievances. First he has to work on the weekend, second he can't trust his wife to pick up her own son from the hospital. So Dave sits in the lobby, without even seventy-five cents to spend on a candy bar at the gift shop. Calls are made to the house, messages left, nurses tsk-tsk and sigh and then finally a St. Mary's nun asks if Dave might have any other relatives he could call.

"Uhm, I'll need the phone book," Dave says, and when a northern New Jersey one is proffered, he says, "Uh, no.

Manhattan." It's Saturday. He calls the Washington Place Diner and Restaurant. A woman answers. She has an American accent, but a cigarette-stained voice. A grown-up.

"I need to speak to Erin," Dave says. "Is she working today? And her father too?"

There's no answer of any sort for a long time. Dave titters nervously and shrugs at the impatient nun. Finally, a younger voice asks, "Hello?"

"Erin, it's me, Dave. I need a ride from the hospital. My parents are, uh, indisposed. I'm being signed out, or I can be signed out, I mean, but I need, uhm, uncle Bill to come get me, okay?"

Erin knows exactly what has happened. It's a perk of her social position as the goddess of discord. She quickly agrees to find and drive out to Hoboken. Then she hangs up without saying goodbye, like in a movie. Dave says "Goodbye" to the dial tone, and tells the nun it will be a while.

It takes hours, but Erin does finally appear, with a grown-up man, a black man. He looks like a newly active volcano, but Erin is entirely carefree, all smiles and twinkling eyes. "Dave!" she shouts, and rushes toward Dave, arms wide for a hug. She strokes his face and fusses over the bandage on his nose, the bloody bruises under his eyes, and the big lump on the left side of his face.

"Hi, Erin . . ." Dave says. And to the man, "Uncle Bill." The nun and a social worker and a nurse appear, happy to sign Dave out to anyone who happens to want him. The social worker nearly asks how exactly haddock-white Dave and swarthy Erin and African-American "Uncle Bill" are related—I can see the word *How* forming on her lips—but she swallows the question. Erin wraps her arm around Dave again and turns him to go, and then she looks over at me. Me, floating in the spaces between quarks, in the froth of the Ylem, and she winks at me.

Moments later they're outside, and without another word the man storms off, muttering about having to get back to work before "the Puerto Ricans rob the store." Dave thinks the man looks familiar—it's the guy who stabbed him with the pen, but before Dave can say anything about it, Erin kisses him on the cheek and whispers in his ear, "I knew you'd come crawling back to me. Don't reject me anymore. I hate it."

Wasn't that the secret theme of *The Iliad*, after all? Jealous Eris creates an apple emblazoned with the legend *Kallisti*. Hapless Paris is then told to choose between Hera, Athena, and Aphrodite, and from his choice comes the Trojan War and the end of the Trojan civilization. But all Paris really had to do was open his eyes, glance over in the direction from whence the apple came, and choose Eris as the fairest. Give her the apple back. Pay her some attention. Is that so much to ask for? In the early twenty-first century, young Erin wasn't even fishing for compliments; she just wanted some company, another member in her secret society. She was looking for Dave, but got me, trapped in the Ylem and visible only to her, forever.

Erin leads Dave down the streets of Hoboken, and it's a small city so there aren't many, and brings him to a Barnes & Noble near the PATH station. They find a loveseat tucked away by the Science Fiction/Fantasy section, and Dave makes a joke about sci-fi fans being the last to need a loveseat and Erin pretends not to get it.

"What do you think your father will do when he gets to the hospital and finds that you've been released into the custody of a non-existent uncle?" she asks.

"I don't want to think about it," Dave says. "Why don't we just go home? If I'm home when he gets home, it won't matter. I'll tell him Mom picked me up."

She ignores that and takes his hand and puts it in her lap. "I want you," she whispers, "to make me come."

Dave squirms away and reaches randomly for a book on the nearest shelf, from the Games section right next to the sci-fi. "Hey, what's this?" he asks himself unconvincingly. The cover's black, with a golden apple on it. "The *Principia Discordia*," he reads, "or *How I Found the Goddess and What I Did To Her When I Found Her*. That's a strange name for a game."

"I think it's fitting," Erin says, and she grabs his wrist and with surprising strength pulls him back down onto the couch. "What would you do to her, Davey? Let's find out. And this will be quick and easy. I told you not to make me mad anymore, not to reject me. Just do it," she says. Her jeans are unbuttoned, the fly halfway pulled down. She takes his hand and flattens his palm against her stomach, then leads it down into her jeans, under her panties, and then lower. "Just rub gently, and you can go home," she says. "I come quick. It's easy. It'll just take . . ." she gasps a bit in his ear, "two minutes." Dave's fingers find coarse pubic hair, and heat, and wet. The blood is swimming behind his eyes again. *If only I had hands with which to pull a fire alarm this time. If only this wasn't the best moment of young Dave's life.* The book falls to the floor. Erin nuzzles Dave's face, his cheek, whimpers into his ear and he massages and prods, sometimes clumsily, sometimes too tentatively. She grunts once, and squirms away from his touch for a moment, but presses his hand back against her sex and grinds against his fingertips. Dave feels for all the world like an innocent bystander in this. His nose still hurts, and it stings when one of Erin's dark curls brushes against his face. But this is his first time really touching a girl. He loves it. He pushes a fingertip into her and is rewarded by a set of slick teeth nibbling on his ear, then a big wet tongue, and a gasp, and a shudder, and a strong hug. Her arms feel like rebar around his ribcage. She wraps her fingers around his wrist, withdraws his hand from her jeans and gently suckles his two wet fingers.

Dave's eyes are wide, like a truck is bearing down on him. He hasn't exhaled in nearly a minute. "Good boy," Erin tells him. "Thank you, I liked that. Did you like that?"

Dave nods.

"Maybe next time you'll let me do you."

"Maybe," Dave says.

"Why don't you go home now? I want to take the ferry back to the city."

"Uhm, okay," Dave says.

"Good, you do that. I'll see you at school on Monday," Erin says as she slips off the couch. She turns a corner around one set of bookshelves and is gone. Dave picks up the book he was looking at, flips through it, and reshelves it before going to the bathroom to deal with his erection. He doesn't make it home in time to get his story straight with Ann, or fool Jeremy. He can hear the howling from the street. Not just his father, but his mother too. Adrenaline and stress must have sobered her up enough to fight back. Dave waits outside till the cops come. It's Detective Giovanni, and a uniform. The detective smiles as he gets out of his car and looks at Dave. "Hey, look! Another missing person case solved." Then his focus shifts to Dave's face. "Blocking punches with your head, eh, Rocky? You need a more active combative strategy."

Dave giggles, but he knows he should be angry.

CHAPTER 16

Dave solves the problem by taking the blame. It was his idea to skip out early, to make up "Uncle Bill," he says. He left Erin out of the story, and inserted Oleg—who probably has a million crazy uncles anyway—in her place. The detective calms his parents. Kids do bad things sometimes, even smart kids, even good kids, if the parents are busy with other things. He studiously examines the wine glasses on the coffee table, even holding them up to the light and sniffing them, though they were all empty except for sticky traces, as he speaks of parental distractions and precarious teenage years. Dave doesn't ask to be excused. He just locks himself in his room and spends the evening sniffing his fingers and dosing himself with Mexican cough syrup, while his computer grinds away in its Napster mp3 downloads.

He wakes up Sunday to the tinkling of a thousand glasses. In the alley between houses, his father is outside, recycling two large Hefty bags full of wine and liquor bottles. Dave sniffs the air. Nothing is cooking, nothing is burning. Not even coffee. Mom must be gone. She is, for a little while. To visit her sister, or some other similar excuse. It's a very quiet Sunday. Jeremy likes to watch golf on TV. They get a pizza and eat half of it for lunch and half of it for dinner. Dave floats the idea of going to the mall and maybe seeing a movie or getting some Dippin' Dots ice cream, but Jeremy thinks a kid who just spent a night in the hospital—"Even if only for observation, and who is sporting a big ol' broken nose"—should relax at home. Get to bed early. School's on tomorrow, no matter what happened last week.

School is a specter haunting the evening, more so than even the Ann-shaped hole in the household. The thought of going back to Hamilton ruins the pizza on Dave's tongue. It deflates every joke on *The Simpsons*. It taints the memory of the bookstore, and the feeling of Erin's sex in his hand. It turns the sprightly theme to *Masterpiece Theatre*—usually Dave's signal to head upstairs to his room for the night because PBS is boring—into a funeral dirge. Dave's surprised that his father is even watching; he'd always assumed that *Masterpiece Theatre* was his mother's show.

The Internet is no help, at first. The songs he downloaded yesterday sound tinny and juvenile. Goth Babe of the Week is a horse-face, and plus all girls look different now that he's actually touched one in a sexual way. It's even more disgusting to look at them, to realize what they want and how they let any asshole with acne and a backwards baseball cap paw at them. The thought of masturbation just reminds him of Erin, which in turn reminds him of school, and the fist in his face, and the sound of his nose pancaking against his skull. He wonders how Oleg is doing, but his friend isn't on AOL Instant Messenger at the moment, and it's probably too late to call. Oleg has an overprotective family—every American has AIDS and deals drugs, you know.

Thinking of Oleg makes Dave think of trench coats, and trench coats suggests Columbine, so Dave Googles that and reads up on the latest news, of which there is very little. Then he types in "assault rifles mail order" and a few dozen pages of links appear. He's just curious. Colorado is a long way from New Jersey, and apparently guns are much easier to get out west. A remnant from the cowboy days, Dave decides. It *is* possible to buy a rifle via Internet, but it's a huge pain in the ass, and one needs to be eighteen years old. It has to be shipped from a licensed dealer to a licensed dealer, and who the hell would hand an awkward-looking kid a submachine gun? In his momentary fantasy, Dave is hoping for a site named something like www.MachineGunsToURDoor. com, with a seven-day free trial on an AK-47 and a no-questions-asked post-massacre return policy.

"That would be cool," Dave says to himself. Downstairs, the TV switches on to *The Sopranos*. "Too bad I don't know any Mafioso," Dave says, again to himself. It's hard to imagine some big Italian guys showing up at a high school to blow away a bunch of high school kids, even if some of them are "moolies," even if some of them are probably in gangs. But Hamilton does have metal detectors, and metal detectors imply the existence of contraband metal objects; and the existence of contraband metal objects means that somehow kids Dave's age can get their hands on guns.

Dave decides that he just needs to put his mind to it.

Poke around. Ask some questions. Cough syrup gives him strength.

But not too many smarts. Lee is laughing at him the next morning. "Oh man!" he cries, "you think just because I'm black I know where you can buy a motherfucking *AK Forty-Seven*!"

Malik is as surprised, but less entertained. "Listen, pussy, just hit the fuckin' gym and lift some weights. Put some muscle on your skinny white ass. You think you're gonna pull a piece on a brother up in here? They'll snatch it out of your hands and punk your ass with it."

Lee suddenly stands very straight and waddles in place, turning to face Malik. With an affected honky accent he asks, "Pardon me, Mr. Negro. Do you think you might be able to assist me in procuring some illegal firearms, so that I may wreak havoc upon your ebony brothers?" Then he collapses into giggles.

"Hey, dudes . . ." Dave begins. Lee laughs even more, snorting out the word *dudes* once or twice between laughs. Malik just shakes his head and pulls out a plastic toothpick. He works it into the gap between his front teeth. "Y'all so fucked up. This fuckin' school is so racist." He walks off, a simmering cloud.

"Anyway, I'm a lover, not a fighter," Lee says. "A heterosexual lover, I mean. Faggot. Anyway, y'all should check in with George. He's a thug, but I don't think he'll sell your white ass a gun. Would you sell him one, if you had one?"

"Well, no," Dave says.

"Why not?"

"Because I'm afraid of him! I'm afraid of everyone,

even you!" Dave says. "But he has no reason to be afraid of me." Dave's up on the balls of his feet, his blood thick with syrup but feeling just that much lighter for it, like he might float away and drift over the Hudson River at any moment, and land at Ground Zero to the applause of the misery tourists. That would be better than another day at Hamilton.

"Yeah, but what if you had a gun? He'd have a reason then."

"Yeah . . . that's why I want the gun."

"'Zactly," Lee says, "that's right." And then the bell rings and they go their separate ways.

Erin isn't in Social Studies. She rarely seems to be in class. Charles is there though, and he's peering at Dave. Dave's just stopped caring and says, in his best imitation of what people have been asking him his whole life, "What are you looking at?"

"Hey, fag, how'd you break your nose?" Charles says. "Some guy thrust too hard in your face at the Mineshaft this weekend?" There are some titters from the class. "Occupational hazard of being a professional cocksucker, eh?"

"I broke it in the fights after the false alarm," Dave says. "Some guy punched me right in the face."

"Yeah, who?"

Dave shrugs.

"Same guy who stabbed you?"

"How'd you hear about that?"

"Word gets around when someone with AIDS starts bleeding all over the school," Charles says. "It was a black guy, wasn't it? Both times, right?"

Dave shrugs again, but doesn't say anything.

"That's a yes," Charles says. "Are you their bitch or something?"

"Yeah, a punk!" some girl says. People turn to look at her; even Charles seems surprised. "I heard that in prison the guys who take it up the ass are called 'punks'," she explains, a little sheepishly. She isn't even affiliated with the Cult of the Shell Necklace, but is confident enough to kibbitz. Dave looks over his shoulders for Mr. McCann, but he's late.

"Man, if one of those 'brothers' tried something like that on me, I'd fuck them up," Charles says. "My older brother was a Dotbuster back in the day." Dave had heard of the Dotbusters—a few dozen kids who used to beat up Indians and Pakistanis up in the Heights.

"Yo, that's bullshit," a kid named Luis calls out. "The Dotbusters were all Spanish, homes. Except for one Polack." Luis holds up a single finger to represent said Polack. "Your family didn't live on no Central Avenue."

"You calling me a liar?" Charles says. Dave takes his seat, happy to be forgotten, almost anxious for some interracial strife. He begins to feel almost giddy, almost the way I do, seeing everyone and everything from the slightest of removes. Maybe it's the long-term effects of the cough syrup, maybe he's just begun to look forward to abuse and beatings, or maybe he just wants to see someone else beaten up for a change. He's on the edge of his seat.

Luis laughs at Charles. "Eat it, man. Just sit there and swallow it." Luis has the mustache of a thirty-year-old and doesn't even bother talking back to teachers to show off. He doesn't need to. Charles decides to swallow it, as recommended, with a shrug and a "whatever." Then to Dave he says, "What are you looking at?"

Dave bursts into rich peals of laughter. He even points at Charles and puts his other hand on his stomach. "Fuck you, man!" Dave shouts. "Fuck you up your ass. You're such a fucking poseur. Tell you what?" Dave says, pointing at his nose. "Punch it."

"I will fucking punch it, if you don't stop fucking laughing."

"Okay," Dave says. He takes ahold of his desk and scoots his chair from its row so that he's closer to Charles. "Go right ahead." He can't stop giggling. Charles doesn't punch him in the nose, but he does slap Dave right across the face. Dave rolls with the blow and cackles, then hops away, still in his seat. Charles jerks his seat with him too, the world's slowest and dumbest chase scene. "C'mon, make me your bitch!" Dave shouts. "Fuck me in the ass!" Then McCann walks in.

"Take your seats," he says. With an eye toward Dave and Charles, he adds, "Back to your rows." McCann doesn't look good—stubbly cheeks, bags under his eyes. Dave giggles and snickers his way through roll call and then another lesson about Latin America. Something about "the disappeared," which Dave thinks is a strange way to put it.

Erin's disappeared, Dave realizes. She usually shows up for at least one or two classes, or lunch, and certainly has a gift for turning the corner at just the right moment and smiling, or scowling, or waving with twinkling fingers at Dave. She's not in school at all today. Did she get sick? Take a bare-assed belt-whipping from her father—isn't that what people from "the Old Country" do to their slutty girls?—or is Erin just avoiding him after the bookstore incident? Because she's embarrassed, or because Dave didn't do a good job with her after all.

Before long, it's lunch, and there is Charles, and James, and a few other of the larger white guys, and they're in a huddle and shooting glances at Dave. So Dave finds George, who is getting himself a whole mess of tater tots and falls into step next to him.

"Hello," Dave says.

George just looks at him.

"Uhm, can I ask you something?"

"I want to ask you something first—what the hell happened to you, dawg?"

"Well, that guy," Dave says, pointing a finger back at James, "punched me in the nose, breaking it, and then the other day when we were all outside with the fire drill, someone else also punched me in the face, so that explains the eye."

"You're a popular kid," George says. He sits in one of the few smaller round tables with freestanding chairs on the far side of the cafeteria—in the "black kid" section. Dave goes to take a seat next to him, but George says, "That seat's reserved," without even looking up from his tater tots. "They're all reserved."

"Oh, well, can I ask you something?"

George shrugs.

"Someone told me that you might know something about self-defense."

George looks at Dave's face. "That makes one of us, eh?"

"I want a gun."

George slaps his hand over his mouth to keep the tater

tots in his mouth from escaping all over the table. He holds up one finger and tries to swallow. Finally, he does. "Aw man, what you need a gun for? Gonna off yourself?"

"For protection," Dave says. "I mean, look at me."

"You'll shoot your eye out, Ralphie," George says. "Ever see that movie? You look like that kid a little bit." Dave thinks that the conversation has attracted some attention, but it's really just George's usual crew, including Lee and Malik and a few girls, standing around the table and watching the spectacle unfold rather than taking their seats.

"This kid wants a gun?" one of the girls asks.

"Remember that fucked-up shit the other day when they brought all the black men in and walked some white kids through to stare at us?" Malik says. "He was one of them."

"I was out that day," George says.

"What was that all about, Damien?" Lee asks.

"Dave," Dave and Malik both say. Then Dave lifts his shirt and shows off his stitches to an appreciative chorus of *daaaamns*. "Someone stabbed me with a pen. For no reason, just came up to me. It wasn't a student, not anyone I recognized anyway. But the principal wanted to get to the bottom of it, so uh . . . I mean, I was totally against it. I'm not a racist."

"Get the boy a medal," the talkative girl says. "He ain't no racist, and now he wants to buy a gun."

"What the fuck, man?" Lee says. He takes a seat opposite George. "Fuck this, I'm eatin'." The others take their seats as well, one girl pushing past Dave and sitting next to George. The conversation is over. Lunch is half-over. Across the cafeteria, the Cult of the Shell Necklace is eating, but still occasionally looking over at Dave, pointing openly and aggressively sipping milk from half-pint cartons. It's a show, and a stupid one, but Dave is a half-pint himself compared to even the smallest cultist, and he's injured and his face begins to throb again. Dave doesn't eat, and he doesn't move. He knows that Charles and his crowd won't dare risk a general confrontation by crossing the imaginary line that separates the races in the cafeteria. At the end of the period, Dave drifts from the black section through to the Latino group and finally attaches himself to the end of the South Asian formation to escape.

I've seen what happens next over and over again. It's like fingering old scar tissue. Dave leaves Hamilton, half-mad, half-terrified. He just wants to go home, get under the covers, and die from the concussion he doesn't even have. What happened to the big lawsuit, to Detective Giovanni? Briefly Dave considers going into Manhattan, to see if Erin was forced to work in the diner after corralling adult help to come get him from the hospital, but he's too tired. He walks home on automatic pilot, limbs working from muscle memory, his mind a worried blank, except for one jejune thought—*How funny it is, Mr. Holbrook, that the guards never try to stop a kid from leaving the school?*

Dave doesn't look back as he walks down the steps. He takes it slow, like the hero in a bad HBO film, and walks purposefully toward a notional movie camera— me, actually, in the Ylem, as I positioned my awareness at the school's gate—and imagines the school going up behind him. Fireballs belch forth from every window, the roof bubbles up and shatters, flaming tiles rain down and litter the street. Then the whole building collapses into its own footprint. If Dave had been wearing sunglasses, he would have whipped them off for effect. Dave is finally free. The marrow of his bones boils with glee.

That's the amazing thing about school. Kids go. Kids who have no interest in learning, who can't learn—they attend. Kids who get picked on, beaten up, groped and robbed in the halls, they show up the next day for more. Dave had taken a creative writing elective the term before and the teacher, a pretty hippie woman named Ms. Reyes, said on the very first day, "And please, no fantasy shoot 'em ups about rampaging down the halls of this school with a machine gun. It's a new day out there, and you won't even flunk the assignment. I'd just have to send you down to the school psychologist." Oleg raised his hand then, and without missing a beat Reyes said, "No, not even if all the other students and teachers have been transformed into zombies or vampires." Oleg put his hand down, defeated.

So Dave got the very top grades in that class, by sitting on the top of the steps, transcribing arguments between his parents as they happened. Reyes loved the pieces because they sounded so authentic, and plus Dave knew the basics of spelling and didn't try to mess with the margins or font sizes in order to meet the four-page minimum for stories.

Dave thinks about that class now, as he walks down Newark Avenue. He has nothing to do, so he heads downhill, almost by instinct, toward the Newport Centre Mall. He can dick around in the small bookstore there, and the game shop, and even check out a movie. It'll be a matinee, and cheap, and he might even be the only one in the theatre. *It'll be like being rich and having a personal screening room in the basement*, Dave thinks. Ms. Reyes was pretty cute, with a wide mouth and deep red lipstick artfully applied each morning. She left Hamilton after a single term, but had to live close by. Maybe she'd be at the movies too, her days free because she had published several poems in literary magazines and royalties were almost certainly pouring in.

Ms. Reyes isn't at the mall. Erin isn't at the mall. It's actually pretty desolate for the early afternoon. Some older white people wander back and forth as though the long arcade of stores is a running track, knots of Indian women and Latinas pushing baby wagons full of purchases chat away happily, and then there are the various workers in their awful synthetic vests, not doing very much at all. They're like school kids, except so beaten down that they don't even have the energy to plot and gossip. Dave feels a surge of power. There's a CVS on the first floor and he decides to get a little cough syrup to make whatever movie is playing upstairs in the multiplex more interesting. And then there's Ann.

"David," she says, surprised.

She sounds odd. *Sober*, Dave realizes. He knows what to say, he thinks. "What are you doing here?"

"What are *you* doing here?" his mother asks. "That's a better question." She's sharp. *She is sober*. Then she looks at Dave's face. The bruise, the bandage over his nose, the something or other in his eyes that unnerves her. "Let's get lunch," Ann says, "then go see a movie."

"Really?" Dave's voice squeaks; it's still breaking. He's a bit of a late bloomer.

She slides her arm into his and leads him to the

cash register. Dave should be embarrassed—normally he would be, like any other teen boy seen out with his mother—but ultimately he's just relieved.

The afternoon is dreamy and odd. Dave even takes a swig of the cough syrup his mother paid for without going through the preliminaries of pretending a hacking cough, a scratchy throat. He's ready for a fight, for a mid-mall meltdown, ready to shout *But you drink all the time, Mom*! but Ann only lightly hmms when he drinks. It's not enough for a physical buzz, but enough for Dave's brain and autonomic nervous system to do half the work. The flavour coating his tongue is the one associated with the drowsiness, the little fever, the colours, and his body obliges even without a full dose. He likes his cheesesteak just fine, and the salty rough-cut fries that come with it, and his mother lets him pick the movie. Samuel L. Jackson is in it, which is enough for Mr. Holbrook, cineaste. The film is even about a powerful hallucinogenic drug that happens to be a placebo, but Dave doesn't get the irony as he sits there and pretends to hallucinate colourful trails on the edges of his own vision. After the movie, they do a little more shopping. Ann treats Dave to a long peacoat. It's not quite a trench coat, but it'll do for winter, and he won't look quite so childlike and weird as he did in his puffy down jacket with the fuzzy hood last year. "Who are you, Ralphie from *A Christmas Story*?" some kid asked him back then before tripping him and sending him headfirst into a pile of grey slush.

And Dave could hide a gun in that coat. Or even a samurai sword. Or, he thinks with a barely suppressed giggle, a large baguette or oversized salami. Robotrippin' makes a man silly sometimes.

Then it's off to Shop Rite for a few groceries, and in Shop Rite there is a separate liquor store. Dave always gets a kick out of it—in New Jersey, supermarkets cannot sell the hard stuff, so some genius emptied out part of the inventory storage area and put in a liquor store with its own cash registers, employees, and employee vests. Ann loads up with her usual wine and vodka, and sends Dave to buy even more orange juice for screwdrivers later.

Later was ten minutes later, back at the house. "Sit," she tells Dave before he can make it up to his room, to his computer.

"I'm sorry I played hooky, Mom, it's just that—"

"Eh, I don't give two hoots about that," Ann says. She's still sober, but her tumbler is the size of a bucket and her drink is a vat of vodka with a splash of OJ. In about five minutes, Dave figures, it'll be all about his mother not giving two fucks. "I wouldn't go to that school either. Not if you paid me. Look at your face!" Then, *sotto voce*, "My poor little boy."

Dave wishes he could pull a swig of his cough syrup, or make himself a screwdriver for that matter, as Ann goes on about how sad and afraid he must be all the time. Does he have a girlfriend, or are all the girls at Hamilton sluts? Dave can't bear to mention Erin—does what he did at the Barnes & Noble in Hoboken count as slutty? By the time Ann's glass is two-thirds empty, she starts.

"It's those niggers ruining everything," she says. "They ruined this whole town. The Hispanics are okay, I guess . . ." Ann always was a lightweight; never had any tolerance for alcohol despite her regular, almost frantic consumption. She mixes herself another and takes a gulp. "Can't leave the orange juice out for long, it'll go sour," she says to nobody.

"White kids pick on me too," Dave says.

"But who broke your nose? Who stabbed you?"

"Who gave me a concussion?"

"That's two against one," Ann says.

"This family is two against one," Dave says. "Just pull me out of school. Homeschool me. Let's move to the suburbs! Do something!"

Ann laughs. "A teenage boy who wants to move to the suburbs." She is really tickled—she *tee-hees* between breaths, and sips. "When I was your age, I was all about the city. I'd go out there and dance all night. All night," she says.

"Gee, Mom, isn't the city full of niggers?" Dave says, snotty.

Ann's face contorts into a sneer. "Fuck you, you pathetic fucking little nerd. I'm sitting here trying to teach you something. Something about life. I don't want you growing up to be a loser; I'm trying to protect you. If I were in school these days, I'd have all those bastards wrapped around my little finger. I used to be good-looking. I was like a short Cindy Crawford." She finishes her second tumbler full of vodka. *At least she'll calm down now*, Dave thinks.

And she is calmer, but she still simmers. "We'll take you out of school. You can go to a Catholic school. Saint John Pope Paul the Second, or whatever the hell that one in the Heights is." She raises a finger. "I don't want you believing in any of that nonsense though. We're Protestants."

"Well," Dave says. "Okay." We were actually entirely irreligious. I never believed in anything, in any timestream save the Ylem from which I deserve all outcomes of my life, where the existence of the supernatural could not be denied. Even the Kallis Episkipos doesn't believe. He just decided that pretending to believe was the same as believing, like pretending to hallucinate is the same as hallucinating.

Dave Holbrook fancies himself a junior scientist of sorts. He earned good grades in his science classes, watched every sci-fi movie that came out, and knew his way around a computer. When he was a kid he read all sorts of books about young boys who tinker with electronics—Danny Dunn, The Mad Scientists Club, Tom Swift—but he lacked the resources to emulate them. No backyard, no friends, no children's world away from the constant surveillance of adults, and no piles of radio gear and lumber left to be nonchalantly discovered and exploited by omnipotent authors. Kids aren't free till high school, just in time for the fucking and the violence and the drug abuse to start.

Back in his room, Dave finishes off his cough syrup. His limbs are heavy; he wants to puke it all up and paint his keyboard purple. He Googles for guns again. There are books, blueprints, suggestions. He could build a gun—if he had a lathe. If he even knew what a shaft collar was. A generation ago, he could have been a tinkerer, like the boys in the books he used to read. He really just wanted something to wave around, something to scare people off with.

CHAPTER 17

Two weeks ago a teenage girl in Youngstown, Ohio scarred her stomach with a razor, then walked out in front of a truck. She was a chub and thus largely intact even after the collision, which was useful for the police because they could more easily identify the design of the cuts on her flesh. Even so, at first the cops thought she had tried to carve herself into a jack-o'-lantern thanks to the jagged-tooth pattern. It was mid-October and Halloween was coming up. Finally, they figured it out that it was the sign of The Resistance, and I got my television interview just in time for November sweeps.

I'm so dangerous it was done via Twitter. I got to tweet, with a hack breathing down my neck behind me, presumably in case I attempted to upload myself to the Internet. Jersey's corrupt enough to let the media do whatever they like with us lifers, but with the cameras flashing the state doesn't want to look *unprepared* or anything.

What do you miss most about life outside?

Eris, the goddess of discord, who walks among you till this very day!

How do you feel when you hear of some naive teenager listening to your garbage and killing herself in such a shocking and public way?

Ladies and gentlemen, that question was from my publicist. Answer: how does the Prez feel when body bags come home?

Do you regret the Hamilton shootings?

Does the Prez regret her war record in Syria?

Do you get it up the ass in prison a lot, you punk bitchfag?

Does the Prez . . . never mind. I'm a giver, not a taker.

Do you realize that you are going to burn in Hell for all eternity, but that the choice remains yours?

False: Typhon, the hundred-headed father of monsters, will consume the universe first.

Also, can people stop asking questions with "do you" in it? Try. Think different, like the billboards used to say.

If you were President, what would be your first act?

Martial law. I always wanted to be popular with the masses instead of my stupid cult following.

Respond to this plz: I hate who steals my solitude, without really offer me in exchange company.

When I declare martial law, I will make it impossible to Google the phrase "Nietzsche quotes."

Look out behind you!

It was a joke so old I had to play it. The hack laid in to me hard. He couldn't help but tweet that tweet, then drop his phone to the floor with a clatter, and try to take my head off with his baton. It took an extraction team to get him off of me. Luckily, there was such a team already stationed outside the door, albeit one whose primary job it was to protect the Fox News laptop and webcam I'd been issued for the interview. So now I am in the infirmary and can make my escape. The hack was a cousin of the fat Ohio girl, so the warden thought he'd be eager to cave my head in. Of course, just like the girl, he was one of mine, just another loser kid from Clifton who busted his ass to get a CO job just to get close to me, to see me go about my day, to make sure none of the other inmates fucked with me too hard.

Vicodin doesn't normally generate hallucinations, but past entertainments have done a number on my kidneys, and it's easy enough to get extra pills, so I can have visions while under the influence. I saw glimpses of my life that one night, what will be and what could have been, but the details were often vague. I know that I'll be free, but not how to be free. If there's a sci-fi paradox in looking into the future to figure out the present, I embrace it, as I embrace all contradictions, all things that sunder logic and reason. Tweet that! So I take my pills, breathe deeply, still my limbs and wait for the latest revelation. I am going to be the man on the glacial throne. I just need to know how I get from here to there.

O

And here it is: what the Kallis Episkipos doesn't know is how his life ends. The drugs don't help him catch a glimpse of me, or any of the other *I's*, as he would put it, this time. Instead he just sleeps and dreams of high school again, like any other arrested adolescent who peaked at sixteen. His confederates continue with their planning—they steal uniforms, bribe orderlies, arrange for a safehouse in the Pine Barrens, and from there an airplane to Florida and a boat to Dominica. Somehow, he—*I*—would get to Marrakech, as Morocco has no extradition treaty with the US. That was the plan. But no, there was no timeline where any Dave Holbrook made it out alive.

So the Kallis Episkipos awakens, the escape plan already mid-execution. He's in a laundry cart being pushed into the yard when he wakes up, but he succumbs to sleep again after a few moments. When he wakes again, the ambulance he's in is roaring down the highway, sirens blaring so intensely that at first he doesn't realize he's hearing the sirens from police cruisers in hot pursuit. Light floods the cabin in bursts—the spotlight from a helicopter, though whether it belongs to the police or the media is beyond him. The Kallis Episkipos gets to his feet just as the ambulance pitches hard to one side and skis on a pair of wheels. Then the police start shooting. He hits the deck and holds on as best he can. He's not sure why the ambulance stops, and it seems a long time before anything happens. A door slams, some muffled orders are barked. Then he hears something at the door to the cabin.

It swings open. He knows the man standing there. It's the detective from years ago, from his high school days. Giovanni—greyer and fatter, but his face as placid as ever. For a moment only. I can smell it on the Kallis Episkipos; he's excited. It must be kismet. The kind detective.

Then Giovanni's eyes widen and he pantomimes a shiver, and shouts, "Gun! He's got a gun!" and reaches for his own sidearm. He plants a bullet in the head of the Kallis Episkipos. Maybe it's the same thick Holbrook skull that saw young Dave through a number of high school beatings, but he—*I*—hangs on for a few moments, just for a few nanoseconds. Giovanni pulls a second pistol from his belt. I feel it pressed into my stiffening hand before the light in this universe goes out entirely.

CHAPTER 18

Dave Holbrook realizes that he needs to take the initiative. That's why Erin has him going so crazy, why he's such an easy target for every racialized faction at school. That's what the gun is, after all—a totem of potency. His *mojo*, still underdeveloped thanks to a slow-ticking puberty. Dave was born toward the end of the year; most of the bullies and jocks and geniuses toward the beginning. Eleven months to catch up on. If only he were still in ninth grade and not tenth.

That's loser talk, Mr. Holbrook, he thinks. Dave is so enamored with his executive functioning, with the mind behind his mind, that he stops for a second, sensing something. Sensing me, in the Ylem, watching him, living him. He shakes it off and without thinking anything else at all, stands up, slips his jacket on and walks downstairs, right past his mother and out onto the streets. To Erin's house. This time, he thinks, he'll be the unpredictable one. He'll be the trickster. And there was the matter of "Uncle Bill" as well. It's only about ten blocks to Vroom Street, and the sidewalks seem to roll Dave toward the building. He even has something to say in case he encounters Erin's father again. *I brought her homework—we're in every class together*. Only at the door to the apartment building, with his finger on the buzzer, does he realize that his line would only work if Erin actually stayed home today. If she cut school entirely and was out wandering around, demanding fingerfucks from other boys or bailing kids out of hospitals, he'd be doomed. He buzzes anyway. Be the trickster, be the wild one.

There's no ritual salutation from the intercom, just a louder return buzz and the *clunk* of a bolt opening up. Something about the immediacy of the buzz says *Erin* to Dave, so he takes the steps two at a time. He knocks on the apartment door and she opens it a crack, peering at him with one eye.

"What do you want?" she says, like he's a stranger.

"We're in a secret society together, remember? Just you and me. What's yours is mine and what's mine is yours, that's what I guess that means." He sees the flesh of her shoulder, creamy save for a pimple or two, and one long hair. Erin doesn't open the door, so Dave says, "Let me in."

"Okay," she says. Erin's wearing pajama bottoms and a blue T-shirt for a restaurant called GYRO PALACE. She turns her back to him to lead him into the apartment, which is cluttered, the walls covered in photos, vaguely Greek statuary and vases on the coffee table and on otherwise barren bookshelves, and he reads the legend on the other side of her shirt: I HAD A GIANT PITA!

"Sick today?" Dave says.

"Yeah, I got a cold." She leaves him standing in the middle of the room and plops herself down on the overstuffed couch. It's the sort of furniture only old people have, and with plastic coverings. Erin puts her feet on the coffee table and flexes her toes. The nails are painted purple. "Did you bring me any homework?"

"I didn't stay in school either today. I'm sick too. We didn't get homework in math for once."

"So you came here to make me sicker?" There's a glass of ice water on the coffee table; she takes it and drinks it down.

"I played hooky and went to the mall. I ran into my mom there, but she was all cool about it because I've been having a hard time lately." He gestures toward his face. "Then we got home, she got soused and started laying in to me."

"Did she buy you that coat?" Erin asks. "It looks cute. Doesn't your friend Trigger have something like it? Why is he named after a TV horse, anyway?"

"Tigger—and there was a horse named Trigger?"

"You know, Roy Rogers."

Dave laughs and sits without invitation next to Erin. "Roy Rogers! How old are you anyway, grandma?"

Erin says, "I have an old soul. All Greeks do."

"Have you ever seen that movie, *My Big Fat Greek*—"

"Yes," she says flatly. "Why are you here, anyway?" She tugs on the hem of his coat.

In a rush, he just says it. "I want you to suck my cock, then I want to fuck you." Before Erin can say anything, the words tumble out of his mouth. "I'm tired of waiting. I'm tired of being teased. You're supposed to like me.

That's why we hang out, isn't it? That's why we did what we did in the bookstore, isn't it? Well, if you can pop in and out of my life, I can do the same to you. That's fair. That's fairness." Then he adds, his eyes locked on Erin's, "And I like you. A lot."

"I have my period," Erin says. Her voice sounds raw, like she really is sick. She takes her glass and gets up without another word, walks into the open kitchen which is packed with shelves—themselves packed with restaurant-sized canned foods—opens the refrigerator, and refills her glass with water from a pitcher. Dave knows he's doomed, but tries to act like a real guy, keeping his eyes on her ass the whole time, though her pajama bottoms are baggy and are a kind of plaid suggestive of an item from the boys' section of a discount clothing store.

Erin comes back to the couch and says, "And fair . . ." She hoists her glass, proposing a toast. "To the fairest!" She clears her throat with a grumbling noise, then gulps down about half her water, letting some of it dribble from the corner of her lips. "You have a lot to learn about women. We're really not so mysterious, but even the most straightforward of girls wouldn't fall for a line like 'That's fairness' when it comes to spreading their legs for a guy."

"I . . . I don't apologize," Dave says. "You're a cocktease, you know that?"

Erin smiles—a thin little line on her face. "Are we breaking up?" she asks.

Dave's face explodes with heat. "We . . . we were together?"

"Were?"

"You're just fucking with me again," he says. "I should slap you across the fucking face."

"Dave, I don't feel well . . ." Erin's voice is light and dreamy now. She stares off at the corner of the room, as though the cobwebs were suddenly intriguing. Dave can't help but be reminded of his mother in that mellow stage between three drinks and five. He really wants to apologize—truly, he should. There's a world in which he does, and it makes him feel better, and he gets a few more weeks of relative peace before picking up a gun and taking it to Hamilton.

"Take your coat off if you're going to stay," Erin says. "Just looking at you makes me feel hot. Feverish, I mean."

Dave shrugs it off his shoulders, but doesn't hang it up. He has nothing to say.

"Are you a member of the Trench Coat Mafia now?" Erin asks.

"Maybe," Dave says.

She leans in close, and whispers in his ear. "Do you have a gun? Do you want one?"

"What would I do with a gun?" Dave says slowly, carefully.

Erin shrugs. "Wave it around. Scare people. Maybe get punched in the face a little less often."

"Get arrested, go to jail . . ."

"Oh Davey," Erin says. "Everyone knows that white kids don't end up in prison for shit like that, unless they actually shoot someone."

"What do you know about guns, anyway? They don't sell them with a side of fries, you know."

Erin squints and licks her lips. "You don't know much."

"It's about that guy, isn't it? 'Uncle Bill'—is he some

criminal you know? Is he going to get me an Uzi?"

"He's not a criminal."

"He stabbed me with a pen."

"It wasn't him."

"How do you know?"

"I know everything," Erin says.

"You're just picking another fight with me," Dave says. "This is stupid." He reaches for his coat.

"Wait," Erin says. She takes his hand. Her own hand is very warm. "I need your help. I'm really not feeling well. Will you go to the bathroom—it's down the hall and to the left—and bring me the cough syrup? It's on the sink, where I left it, I think. No need to look through the medicine cabinet, understand?"

"Okay, sure," Dave says. And he goes, and the cough syrup isn't on the sink, so naturally he looks in the medicine cabinet for it. It's there, *sans* label and in a glass bottle rather than a plastic one. And he sees an assortment of pill bottles. He takes a look, but the prescription information is all in Greek. He tries to figure out whether the name "Erin" appears anywhere—*E is the same, isn't it, and doesn't the Greek r look like an English p*? But maybe Erin wasn't even her real name. Her real Greek name.

"What's taking so long!?" Erin calls out to him from the living room. Dave takes a swig of the cough syrup— it tastes odd, like something old and licorice-y—and brings it into the living room. He'd half-hoped that she would have her pants off or something similar, but no. She held out her arms and wiggled her fingers like a baby. "Thank you, thank you!" she says as she takes the bottle and drinks from the cap. "Thanks again."

Dave sits back down. Erin passes him the bottle. He swigs right from it, without bothering to use the cap. They pass the medicine back and forth for a while, not saying anything, but enjoying the touching of their knees, the brushing of finger against palm.

"Why do you think people pick on you?" Erin finally says.

"I dunno," Dave says. "They can, I guess. They pick on Tigger too, but not as much."

"Because he's a little crazy-looking."

"And there are a few Armenians in the school. Some big guys—they're like trucks who wear sweaters. They're all tight."

"And you got nobody, eh?" Erin says.

Dave giggles. "I got you, babe . . ." he says, voice a sing-song.

"And I got myself a gun," she says, another melody.

"Why all this gun talk?" Whatever Dave's been drinking, it's not over-the-counter. His blinks are longer than his looks.

"You think you're the only one being attacked?" Erin says, that edge back in her voice. Or maybe the cough syrup doesn't coat her throat quite as well as it could. "Why do you think I enrolled in that shitty school? Why we're living out here in *Joisey* instead of Astoria in this dump above some third-cousin's luncheonette?"

Dave doesn't have anything to say to that. Is it another wind-up to a joke only Erin will ever get?

"Whatever . . . it was a rhetorical question," Erin says, finally upset about something. Angry rather than mocking. Defeated instead of enthusiastic. Petulant and not scintillating. From the Ylem I scream *It's a trap*!

and Dave does get a sense of foreboding, but he doesn't listen.

"Why don't you get a gun, then?"

"I have two already," she says. She struggles to get off the couch and again walks to the kitchen and then through a small door Dave hadn't noticed before. A few moments later, she returns with a pair of very real-looking guns. Uzis, just as he had said. "Minis. Easy to hide in a coat like that."

"Machine guns?"

"Of course not. These are sub-machine guns. They use pistol ammo."

"Where did you get them?"

"When you have family in the restaurant business in New York, you just get to know people, you know?" Erin says.

"Are those legal?"

Erin stares at Dave as though he, in the space of a breath, had developed Down's Syndrome. "No. Nor is taking them to school and waving them around. This is a Bonnie and Clyde gig."

"Who?"

"Sid and Nancy?"

"Still nuffin', sorry," Dave says. His tongue is beginning to feel leaden.

"Mickey and Mallory?" Erin says.

"Oh, okay," Dave says. "But no killing, right?"

Erin sits down next to Dave again, the guns heavy in her little hands. "I don't think either of us have that in us."

And in a way, Erin's right. She's never done her own dirty work. Not in the beforetimes when the world was

young and Zeus faced down Typhon with the victory
goddess Nike at his side and Eris on the side of the
great hundred-headed dragon, not in Greece where she
chucked an apple into a party to which she was not
invited, and not now either.

And she's right about Dave Holbrook, in most cases.
I couldn't have done it. I still wonder if that's why, with
a flick of the wrist and a blanket, she exiled me here. The
one who did it hardcore, he was able to spread discord
after a fashion with his "movement" of malcontents, but
in the great scheme of things, all those high school goons
didn't add up to much more than a handful of suicides,
one copycat stabbing spree by a kid in Massachusetts
who couldn't get his hands on a gun, and a pop culture
footnote of less import than Charles Manson. Someone
somewhere made enough money on those resistance
symbol stickers to buy a small house in Berkeley,
California's worst neighbourhood, but that's about it.

Erin never does show up that day, though. Dave
does. He decides that he's going to, right now. He won't
brandish the gun, he says to himself, unless someone
starts something with him. Then he realizes that
someone starts something with him nearly every damn
day. So he won't take it out unless someone pulls a
weapon, or if he ends up on the floor of a hallway, books
scattered everywhere. But what if the gun goes off from
the impact? There's a safety on it, sure, but . . .

"We should go someplace and practise shooting
these."

"You want to practise shooting machine guns?" Erin
asks.

"Yeah, we can do it in the swampy area by the Liberty

Science Center. Shoot over the river or something. It's not like the bullets will make it to Manhattan."

"Yeah," Erin says, suddenly bright. "And if they do, it'll just blend in with the criminal weather over there."

"Yeah, who'd even notice?"

They kiss. For quite a while. But they keep their hands on their guns.

CHAPTER 19

There's only one world where Dave and Erin go out to practise. What Dave didn't know, as he didn't read the papers much, is that the "swampy area" he recommended was to become Liberty National Golf Course. It was still three years from opening when he and Erin took their Uzis out to practise, but there was some construction going on. Security was present. Calls were made. Sirens blared. A police boat roared into view right off shore. Dave froze. Erin vanished. On a flat plane, tens of yards from any building or hole in the ground, she just disappeared, leaving her Uzi in the muddy ground to annihilate any fingerprints. Dave ran for it, ditched the gun, and actually managed to get away. The gun he had left behind somehow ended up in his locker, and a janitor popped the lock when a trail of mud leaked out from the bottom of the locker and onto the floor. Dave's solution was elegant—he burst into hysterics in the principal's office, snatched a letter opener off the desk right in front of Doctor Furgeson and plunged it into his own neck.

But *Mr. Holbrook* isn't in that world. In this world, there's no practice session. Dave doesn't take a gun home with him. He leaves Erin's after some making out so as to avoid meeting her father on the steps again. He doesn't take one of the Uzis with him because that would be insane. Only after walking halfway home does he realize that he never got an answer about the mysterious "Uncle Bill," and that his virginity is still intact. Why did she kiss him if she had her period? Why not at least offer to jerk him off?

"Wouldn't that be the polite thing to do?" he mutters to himself. To me. I don't answer, but perversely I want to whisper something about fairness in his ear.

The difference between the world where Dave and Erin march out across knee-high grass to shoot guns at Manhattan and all the others is that tonight Jeremy doesn't come home. He often stays late at work—why wouldn't he?—but never has he just gone missing. Ann is beside herself. She fills up his work voicemail and his cell phone, wonders aloud if she should call the police.

"I think it takes forty-eight hours before one can file a missing person report," Dave says.

"How do you know?" Ann says, her voice a whip.

Dave shrugs. "TV."

"Pfft." Ann is agitated, pacing across the living room. Everything smells like booze and perfume. "I don't want a missing person report. Your father didn't run off!"

"He didn't?"

Ann ignores that. "He's probably been in a car accident, or is stuck on the turnpike somewhere. I want the police to call the state troopers and run his plates." She has a wine bottle in one hand, the phone in the other. "Is this a 911 call?" she asks herself. "Dave, get the phone book. Find the precinct number."

Ann can't bring herself to make the calls. She pours a glass to steady her nerves, then another. She debates with herself—should she call the JCPD or the New Jersey State Police? What was the damned license plate number, anyway? How come Dave, who is so smart and has such a great recall, didn't memorize it either?

She finally decides to call the state troopers and is caught in their endless phone tree. "What if this were an emergency?" she sputters into the phone. Then she laughs at herself. "I guess I'd call 911 if it were, eh?" She winks at Dave. "Can you get on the other line, the one you use for the computer, and order us some pizzas? I think that'll be our dinner tonight, okay? Will that make you feel better?"

It will not. Dave makes the call, then gets on the computer. There's little to do but check the news and look at pictures of bodies mangled in wrecks. A complete jaw topped by a pile of what looks like smashed watermelon. A pair of legs on the street. He thinks to call Erin. She knows criminals. She has guns in her kitchen. And he wants to talk to her. But when he calls, the phone just rings and rings—no pick-up, no answering machine.

Dinner is in the living room, sullen and quiet. The pizza tastes like ketchup'd cardboard, and every pair of headlights that shine through the curtains must be Jeremy's car. And when there are no cars, Ann still parts the curtains to frown at the empty street. There's no news of a car accident or a pile-up on the turnpike on the 9 o'clock news, nor the 10 o'clock news, nor on 1010 WINS, which Ann makes Dave tune into via the old battery-operated transistor radio he got in advance of a promised camping trip that never happened. Ann declares that she'll sleep on the living room couch tonight, and will smack Jeremy with her slipper when he finally walks through that goddamn door, and Dave has nothing to do but go to bed.

For a long time, Dave does not sleep. He doesn't even worry about school the next morning, or fantasize about sneaking Uzis past the metal detectors, or think overmuch about Erin. His father's absence is troubling, much more so than he ever thought it would be. Ann will have a meltdown if the morning brings another cop to the door, this one with bad news. She can't work. They'd lose the house. Maybe Dave would have to go all the way down to North Carolina and live with Grandma, in her double-wide trailer home. Without Dad, maybe he would end up a real street kid, and finally toughen up. He'd have to wear an itchy suit to the funeral. There would be hugs, and tears, and they'd be a million times worse than the ones rolling down his cheeks right now.

Finally, he sleeps. One interesting thing about Ylem is this: as I am conscious of every moment of every possibility of my life, I have unfettered access to my own dreams. We don't really remember our dreams so much as piece them together in the moments after waking. Dreams aren't much more than flashes, montages from a dozen different films. And sometimes—and this might just be because Dave Holbrook is here in the Ylem forever—those flashes come true.

Dave dreams of a woman, white and skeletal, dragging herself out of the black earth. Where she goes, war follows.

Dave dreams of a life in the alleyways, a cold spike of fear embedded in his spine. Eating garbage to live.

Dave dreams of Erin, his fingers in her sex, her eyes shut and mouth open.

Dave dreams of a kid in school, his hands up and screaming, tears everywhere.

Dave dreams of the man who stabbed him, of the man who signed him out of Saint Mary's with Erin and then left without a word. He had seen him a third time too—the first time, actually—in the Washington Place Diner and Restaurant. *The short order cook*! His eyelids fly open for a moment, and he sees his father, Jeremy, looming over him, a shadow.

No, not Jeremy, someone else. *Me*.

Dave dreams of me, just as the Kallis Episkipos wanted to. He sees me, but he does not know me. I see him, and I know him, but can't reach out and touch him, or speak to him, or tell him not to be stupid. Live the boring life of a state employee. Go ahead and spend two decades jerking off to Internet porn and end it all by accident one night with a cheap plastic belt. A belt that was supposed to snap and didn't. Be glad it didn't.

Dave dreams of other things. The dog he wanted as a kid. The one he created in his imagination after his parents woke him up one morning at five in the morning and pushed him outside into the freezing rain. "You'll have to wake up this early every morning and walk the dog if we got you one," Ann had said. She was in her robe. Jeremy was already dressed for work. He said nothing, but stood behind his wife and nodded like a stranger agreeing with an overheard conversation. He dreams of a comic shop where all the covers are exciting and blindingly colourful, but when he opens up the pages he can't read the dialogue in the balloons. He dreams of the smell of frying bacon, of a long-nailed hand against his bedroom window, of five white lines being scratched into the glass, of his mother howling when she finds them.

At three in the morning, Dave hears something and falls out of REM sleep. Jeremy passes by the bedroom door on his way to his own bedroom. Downstairs, on the couch, Ann snores loudly.

O

If there's a discussion regarding Jeremy's whereabouts, Dave isn't a party to it, and he's not allowed to ask where his father had been all night. Ann hisses like a snake when he tries. Jeremy isn't sporting a black eye, and all his teeth seem to be in place—though Dave is still happy to consider a criminal underground of midnight dentists, somewhere out there in the world of diabolical adults— and indeed Jeremy even seems content. He whistles as he butters his English muffin. Ann's nursing a headache with a mimosa and a wet washcloth at the kitchen table. Finally, Dave realizes that his father has probably been to see a whore. He's both upset and strangely aroused. It would be some news to share with Erin anyway, something to talk about other than Uzis.

After homeroom, there's a surprise assembly. Seniors are excluded "because the damage has already been done," according to Oleg, who squeezes into the tight auditorium seat next to Dave, who had scored himself an aisle. "It's anti-bullying stuff. Haha!" he says. Dave spots the black puff of Erin's hair somewhere a few rows down and decides that he will stare at her until she turns around, thanks to his awesome mental powers.

"How do you know?"

"I have my ways."

"And they are?"

"I saw some guys bringing in the projection screen and some film canisters by the loading dock. There's also some old lady dressed like a cheerleader or something."

"I didn't even know this school had a loading dock."

"Sure," Oleg says. "How do you think they get desks and equipment and bullshit in—through the front-door metal detector?"

Dave's mind spins. At that moment, Erin turns around to look at him—her eyes are the opposite of headlights, two dark pools under the bright lights of the auditorium. The lights dim.

It's an hour of footage from CNN's Columbine reportage, of clips from popular films about young kids standing up for themselves against unarmed bullies. Backpacks and clean, undented lockers are everywhere. The kids have late-model cars and lean up against them casually as they insult a gallery of hapless nerds. "A lot of white-on-white crime in Hollywood," Oleg whispers into Dave's ear. "Everywhere on TV is the suburbs," Dave says, "except in music videos."

Then the cheerleader comes out, with two big guys in sweater vests and button-down shirts. "It's like we've fallen into a timewarp," Dave says. "Greetings, time travellers from 1953!"

Dave didn't pay too much attention to the skits, but he did enjoy the round of echoing boos that filled the auditorium when the two sweater guys dared to start rapping. Mostly he just daydreamed about someone else strolling in from backstage, machine guns blazing, and shooting the first ten rows into meat sauce. The survivors trample one another on the way out, only to find that the doors have been chained shut. Then the smoke starts to pour in from the vents. *No wonder they didn't announce the assembly in advance*, he thinks.

In the dark, he can't see Erin anymore. She taps him on the shoulder and he practically jumps out of his seat. "C'mon," she says, crooking a finger. Oleg follows without an invitation, and if Erin has any magic in her glare, he's proof against it. "You know I'm coming with you!" he says. "Don't even think about leaving me alone in this place, without entertainment."

The boys make to head up the aisle, but Erin grabs their sleeves. "All the doors are guarded. This way." She leads down toward the stage, and toward a trap door under it.

"What the—"

"Back in the old days, this school had an orchestra," she says. "And an orchestra pit." Dave helps her lift the door, and she slides down the four-rung ladder. Oleg squeezes into the space as best he can, and from the ladder holds the door open for Dave.

Erin strikes a match and holds it up to her face. The flames flicker in her eyes, and she looks like an ancient thing. It's a face not meant to be illuminated by electricity at any hour of the day or night, but one to be cut by a slice of moonlight, one to emerge out of gloom and fog. Sharp cheekbones, coal eyes, her mouth a wave.

"Follow me if you want to live," she says. She snorts. Erin doesn't giggle. Dave does.

What Erin has to show them is a whole other school. She lights matches and lets them burn to her fingertips as she leads them under the stage, into the storage areas. Manual typewriters piled high against one wall; a web of ancient iron-legged desks thrown together in one corner, complete with inkwells and penknife graffiti by teens likely dead by now; ropes from a boxing ring in another corner; a large cardboard and rat-chewed megaphone with the letter H stamped on one side.

"This school used to be cool," Oleg says.

"Where are we going?" Dave asks.

"There's a ton of stuff down here," Erin says. A match goes out. She lights another. Oleg crushes the old one under his heel. "We don't have anything like this anymore."

"We don't need it. We have a computer lab. And it's not like you guys care about pep rallies and taffy pulls all of a sudden," Dave says.

"Taffy pull!" Oleg waggles his eyebrows. Nobody laughs. Erin walks ahead, and the boys follow. "Which way to Freddie Krueger?" Oleg asks himself, and nobody laughs a second time. Dave thinks that he and Erin could be having sex down here if not for his friend—maybe on the four-wheeled cart holding up the skeleton of a parade float, or maybe on the stack of blue wrestling mats turned grey by dust and dark and age. It would be awkward, and short, and there might be a wayward elbow to the face, but it would be something. Something like his father might have been up to at a rest stop on the turnpike last night with a stranger in a miniskirt and a mink stole. That's what Dave always imagined hookers looking like.

Dave nearly walks into something, and calls for the match to be brought closer. "It's a printing press of some sort, I guess." He finds an E among the jumble of sorts in a little wooden box on his very first try and presents it to Erin. "For you."

"Thanks," she says a little awkwardly. "I'm running out of matches."

"Well, what did you want to show us?" Oleg says.

"Us," Erin says, without affect. Then she says, "All of this, I suppose. What the school could have been like. A school paper, sock hops, boy cheerleaders like upstairs in that insipid assembly. Those computers you like, Dave, are old pieces of shit—"

"I know it," Dave says. "And dial-up on most of them."

"But this stuff was high-quality educational material back in the proverbial day," Erin says. The match goes out again, and she lights yet another. Dave sees for the first time that she has an entire box of long kitchen matches in her little purse. Likely from the diner, he supposes. "Even now," she says over the sizzle of the burning match, "it's like nobody can bear to throw any of this stuff away. I was down here a couple of days ago—I even saw some film cameras. Real film, not video."

"That's pretty cool," Oleg says. "We could still use those!"

"Stop-motion animation," Dave says. "We could get action figures and . . ." and Dave remembers that Erin is right next to him and swallows his enthusiasm.

"Everything that's good they take away from us. Always," Erin says. There's a rumble from above. "The assembly is letting out. Let's get back upstairs before they see that we're missing."

"Who'd miss us?" Oleg says.

"Us," Erin says again, flat as a dead man's electrocardiogram.

"I'm taking one of these," Oleg says, and he holds up an ancient film camera like it was a pistol. "Long coat, big pockets." He slips it under his leather duster. Dave had left his coat in his seat.

"I wonder if they even make film for that anymore," Dave says.

"They probably don't," Erin says.

Oleg hangs around for lunch too, a fifth wheel who thinks he's the first. He either doesn't get that Erin's clipped responses mean that she's simmering with rage, or doesn't care. Dave can't eat, though the cafeteria is quiet for once. No fights, no shouting, no sudden spray of milk, or cruel laughter and hooting.

"Do you think the assembly worked?" Dave says.

"Doubt it!" Oleg says. "People are just happy to be out of that assembly. That was some mind-numbing shit, even compared to class. Right?" he says. "Right?" he says again, looking at Erin. There's breading from fish sticks all over his lips. "So, are you two a couple?" he says.

"Uhm . . ."

"No," Erin says. "He just fingered me once."

Oleg laughs, half-shocked, half-thrilled. He waves his arms just like a cartoon tiger, and the first half-pint of milk of the afternoon flies.

Dave finds a note in his coat pocket after lunch. It's from Erin—even her handwriting is sharp and pointed, not full of swirls and curly-cues like that of most girls her age—and it reads *Meet me later. You know where.*

BULLETTIME

O

She doesn't come. *She's not coming, Mr. Holbrook*, Dave thinks, alone in the dark, and though he is sad and worried, he chuckles over his mental pun. The old wrestling mats in the basement of Hamilton High School aren't nearly as soft as he imagined them. Good thing he imagined Erin on the bottom, and him on top, pumping like a jackrabbit. Dave has clearly gone insane; the lingering sulfur scent of Erin's kitchen matches remind him of her, and how much he wants her. He's a colour wheel of emotion from here in the Ylem—every creek and thud is her, and so he is exultant for a half-second at a time. Then miserable. Was this another joke? Another lie? Then suddenly worried—*Erin must have tried to load the Uzis and shot herself in the face!* Hair and bone embedded into the white walls of her living room, the top of her head missing like someone had taken a bite out of it. He had no cough syrup with him, but he managed to calm himself, anyway.

After a while, Dave gets antsy, and I try my best to keep him down in the basement. *Fuck this, I need to go home. I'll call her at home*, he thinks and I whisper in his ear, *Five more minutes; she'll be pissed if you're gone when she comes.* He needs to pee, and I tell him to be a man and hold it. Dave grows bored, and I tell him to find something to steal, like Tigger did. Something even cooler, like an old Radio Shack computer, or maybe some student records from the 1940s, if he could find them. I just need to give Erin some time, maybe a half hour at best, but it doesn't work. Dave heads back up the ladder into the auditorium, and finds his way out to the loading dock. The door near the dock entrance is locked, but not from the inside.

O

Dave hears it before he sees it, but it sounds so strange that he can't help but walk up the little three-step stoop, put the key in the front door, open it, walk into the vestibule, and then open the door to the living room. And there she is, live as porn. Erin, naked, straddling Jeremy, but facing away from him in a reverse cowgirl position. Her breasts are plump and pointed, nipples huge, her eyes wide open and staring, bush black and trim, her mouth like an O. Behind her, Dave's father sits naked and fleshy, his hands on her tiny waist, his pants pooled around his ankles.

"Don't fucking stop!" Erin says, her voice feral. She reaches back and slaps Jeremy as best she can with her chicken-winged arm. "Keep fucking me!" Dave just opens his mouth and vomits.

Jeremy throws the girl off of him and steams forward awkwardly as he pulls up his pants. "David! You get the hell out of here!" he bellows. Dave pedals backwards into the vestibule, and his father slips right on the puddle of vomit and falls atop him. Erin's stomping around, picking up clothes, cursing in two languages. "Where's mom! Where's mom!" Dave demands. He's sure Erin's killed her, or maybe Jeremy did. "How do you two even know each other!" He can't stop staring at the condom on his father's penis. It looks like a grocery bag that had been left in the gutter.

Erin hops over Jeremy, who is in tears now, beating

his vomit-stained fists against his own thighs, and shoulders Dave out of the way. She mutters, "Excuse me," as she does, and Dave can't help but flash back to James. His nose hurts all over again. Everything does. He has nowhere to go, so he runs to his room.

Dave slams the door shut behind him and pulls on the corner of his cheap four-drawer bureau till it falls across the door. That'll keep his father out—he's expecting bellowing and fists against the door, but nothing is forthcoming. He dumps the contents of his book bag on the floor and starts grabbing clothes and stuffing them in it. Ann isn't around, but he's sure she will be soon, to come and pick him up. Maybe not one hundred percent sure, but it seems like a reasonable expectation. If not, he can stay with Oleg for a few days.

Dave realizes that he's never been to Oleg's house. He's not even sure where in Jersey City Oleg lives, though it has to be fairly close to the school, and JC simply isn't that big of a town. He drops the bag to the floor. Oleg isn't a good friend, Dave finally figures out. He's a lunchroom buddy and a hanger-on—a sidekick. Or maybe Dave is the sidekick. Oleg comes and goes as he pleases, and basically shows up whenever he needs an audience. He's not picked on as severely as Dave, and even threw down during the altercation outside the school, for all the good it did.

But it's not as though Oleg ended up spending a night in the hospital. It's not as though Oleg's breath always smells cherry-sweet from all the Robitussin. *Though the boy could use some mouthwash, Mr. Holbrook*, Dave thinks. Maybe Oleg couldn't—or wouldn't—take him in because of his fussy Old World parents.

Dave's next thought is for Erin, but all he can see now is her tits hanging off her slim torso, her pubes, how her face looked with his father's bagged dick inside her. He gets on the computer and starts frantically Googling for anything. Youth hostels are for eighteen and up; turning himself in to the foster care system would be insane and certainly wouldn't be any safer than Hamilton. Hitting the streets just sounds dangerous—maybe the Hare Krishnas in the East Village would take him in, but Dave can't stand the idea of vegetarianism, or brainwashing. He's not coming out of his room without a plan, but he already failed to make one. He has no food up here. Not even a candy bar in his book bag. He could call for pizza, but doesn't have much cash on him, and there's no way he could convince the delivery guy to hop the fence, come around to the backyard, and then clamber up on the shed and stretch really hard to hand over the mozzarella sticks.

Maybe Dad will leave too, and I'll be alone. Dave couldn't pay the mortgage, or the power bills, but he has ninety days before they're turned off. Unless Ann was already late in paying the bills, which she frequently was. That's a dumb fantasy. Then there is Hamilton's storage area, but the dust and mould would probably give Dave asthma, and besides, Erin knows all about it. That's the first place she'd look, if she wants to rub his face in all that she has done. She spread her legs and that hairy twat for his own father.

Dave can't think anymore. He can almost feel his brain shutting down. I can feel it too; I feel it every time I revisit this moment, and I revisit it frequently. There's a great, if momentary, gap where David Holbrook's consciousness used to be. His body incapable of anything else, he collapses onto his bed. And he hits something hard under the comforter.

Erin had left the guns for him to find. Dave starts thinking again.

CHAPTER 20

In the Ylem I can live an infinity of my own lives. I've been the baby howling in the light, covered in blood and goop, feeling my own limbs for the first time. I've been myself finally realizing that there was a person behind the pair of boobs I sucked on four times a day. I can relive my first cookie, my first erection, the first time I was by myself in a car, driving down the turnpike without either parents or passengers to keep me from singing along with the radio—all of it is mine to live and live again. What prison food tastes like. How someone's face just stops moving the moment after the body dies. The smell of Erin's hair that first time. The smell of her fucking that last time.

But there are many things I'm not a party to. I've grown up here in the space between spaces, in the moments between seconds, and I've learned a lot about myself, from myself. We are more than just our thoughts and feelings. There are deeper impulses we can never access, and they come from somewhere else. Maybe it's epigenetics—one Dave eats lots of Pop-Tarts and the chemicals influence his brain chemistry sufficiently that he becomes a happy mass murderer. Or maybe Ann snuck a few drinks during her third trimester and that ruined some of me.

One time, when I was eight years old, an old shopkeeper threatened to cut my dick off for stealing when he saw me trying to pocket a Mounds Bar; in another timeline he didn't and I got away with it. The first Dave was awkward and shy and ran crying from Erin that evening in Hoboken. He ended up killed in a fire in a shitty Union City apartment at the age of twenty-two. The second was the one who just discovered two loaded Uzis in his bedroom. I can't see all the dots, and those I can see I cannot always connect with confidence. So many Daves, knees weak and stomach empty, threw themselves back-first onto his bed, but only three took up the challenge of the gun.

Dave wisely didn't try anything the next morning. He wakes up to a home empty except for a twenty-dollar bill on the kitchen table, with a Post-It note reading FOR FOOD!! attached to it. No messages on the machine from his mother either. Dave takes a look around the house to see if he can find any other money, and manages to score another fifty-seven bucks from his mother's dresser, plus a handful of quarters and gold dollars. He tries wearing the Uzi too, but reconsiders it for two reasons—his new wool coat actually doesn't obscure it well enough, plus everyone is likely on edge due to yesterday's assembly.

Mr. Holbrook, he thinks as he fills a shot glass with cough syrup for breakfast, *was yesterday's assembly about you? Or are lots of kids being beaten up in the halls?* Maybe someone else would bring a gun to school, or a pipe bomb, or even hijack a plane with a soda can in a thick sock and try to slam it into the place. Hamilton was just big enough to get lost in, but not so big that Dave could avoid his tormenters. Maybe those other nerds from the racist cafeteria line-up had holes in their sides from pen-wounds too. Or maybe they just had richer, more together parents with school board members on speed dial.

No Erin in school. Dave isn't surprised. What is surprising is another assembly, right after homeroom.

"There's gonna be a week of this shit," Lee tells Dave. It was an awkward rush to the auditorium today, so Dave just squeezed in anywhere, and Lee surprised him by plopping down next to him. "No homo," Lee says.

Dave's so used to it, he ignores the insult and carries on with the conversation. "How do you know?"

"My auntie's on the district school board," he says. "I'm gonna have to fly right. That's why I'm sitting here with you, instead of my crew. If Hamilton don't straighten up, they gonna bring in a bunch of crazy Vietnam vets to be the teachers and make us wear uniforms like Catholic schools do."

"Is that even legal?" Dave asks, but the lights dim and Lee decides to concentrate on the stage rather than answer.

This time the assembly is by the JCPD. Detective Giovanni stalks the stage like a TV preacher, bellowing into a microphone, promising swift vengeance and hinting at a decade of daily prison rape should anyone engage in gang activities or bullying. "It's *assault*!" he shouts. "Assault and battery!" There are no Hollywood movie clips or dance numbers, but there is a brief scare film about a young girl whose brother was shot and killed, and how much she misses him. Some grainy photos of the boy are flashed on the screen—he's an obvious acolyte of the Cult of the Shell Necklace. The black and Latino kids chuckle and hiss, and even Dave smirks.

"That guy looks like a total asshole," he whispers to Lee, but Lee ignores him. Instead, Lee says, "I don't know why I'm here. Black people don't shoot up schools. They could have put us all in the cafeteria again and shown your white ass this movie."

Dave realizes that if he does bring the gun to school, he might have to shoot Lee first. And Malik. That George guy as well. Just because he foolishly asked them if they knew where to get guns.

The assembly is short enough, but afterward Vice Principal Fusco takes to the stage and announces that there will be assemblies every day for the rest of the week. Tomorrow, Wednesday, will be on sexual harassment. Fusco bellows the word *sexual* as though daring the students to hoot or giggle. Thursday will be on the new dress code. "Not uniforms, but a dress code. Proper, professional dress. No more baggy pants or midriff-bearing blouses or gang colours . . . like blue or red." That summons up some murmurs of protest. It's pretty hard to avoid blue. Then there's Friday's assembly, which will involve the mayor, and a "famous rap star"—more buzzing, now positive—and "lots of media and security."

Friday will be too intense. Thursday it will be. He cuts class after the assembly in the usual manner of leaving school for lunch and then just continues to walk. Nobody's home, but now the answering machine is full of messages. The first is from Ann, obviously inebriated and a little giggly, insisting that Jeremy take a leave of absence from his job to "care for poor Davey." The next is from Jeremy, demanding that Ann call him at work to demonstrate that she is "ready to be a mother, if not a wife." Neither of Dave's parents are clever enough to actually check their messages from afar, even though Dave has drilled them on how to do it a million times. Ann left three messages in a row after Jeremy's—the first two are increasingly angry, and in the third she's calm again, as if having been reset. Jeremy's last two messages are short. The last is just him saying, "Call me! Now!" as best he can through clenched teeth.

Dave waits on the couch, thinking. Barge in blasting, or hide the gun in the basement. He has two—he can do both, or either. He only has four magazines, so it might be best to keep the guns separated so he doesn't blow all his ammo doing a *Scarface* routine. He barely even notices that the plan has shifted from *waving the guns around with Erin* to *actually shooting people*. And he wants to live. Running out of ammo and letting the cops shoot him is not an option. He could run, or surrender, or just not do it.

No, there is no *just not do it* anywhere in Dave's head. Early-onset schizophrenia, maybe. Stress from both his parents leaving him, perhaps. The influence of the goddess of discord seducing Jeremy and fucking him right on the couch, the couch that is still stained with something, that still smells like her, that last and final betrayal.

His nose still hurts. It's hard to breathe. There won't be much running on Thursday. Around 4 p.m., he reaches over to the phone and makes a call.

"Tigger," he says when Oleg answers.

"Cutting again, eh?" Oleg says. "Slippin' Erin the ol' baloney pony?"

"Wait . . . what?!"

"What what?"

"If I were doing that, why would I call you right after?"

"That was going to be my next question!"

"Anyway," Dave says. "Remember that time you found me bleeding in the bathroom?"

"A mother always remembers her daughter's first period, David."

"Be serious. You said something about teaching those dirtbags a lesson. I wonder if—"

"Yes!" Oleg says. "I'm all for it. My brother Aram got Photoshop. I say we start a website and stick the heads of our tormentors on some gay porn pics."

"Where are you going to get gay porn?"

"Google. What, you mean you've never even peeked?"

"Uhm . . . anyway, I have a better idea." It's not a better idea. Dave says he needs a kilt, and needs to borrow Oleg's duster in order to better reveal it at the right moment. Oleg says he'll leave it on Dave's stoop, secret agent-style. Dave doesn't bother to explain that secret agents don't leave thing on stoops.

"Shave your legs too!" Oleg says.

Nobody came home that night. Dave's choices were to moon over Erin, to gnash his teeth and chew on his fingers and chant "Cunt! Cunt Cunt!" through clenched teeth—just like his father spoke to his mother—till his lips bled, or to think about Hamilton, and what he could do with those Uzis.

Maybe Erin will show up. Maybe she fucked Dad just to

gain entry to my room and leave me the guns. Like Mata Hari or La Femme Nikita . . . he thinks, but then it's back to slapping his palms against his temples, then back to reading up on school shootings.

He could just shoot Erin, he supposes. If not at school, then on the way to school. Drop by her apartment and plug her. Her fat obnoxious father too. Maybe go to the city and visit Washington Place Diner and Restaurant and put a bullet in "Uncle Bill"—who did look just like the guy who had stabbed him with a pen.

Revenge is hard work. Dave knew the old saying, *Before you embark on a journey of revenge, dig two graves.* He had lots to dig, and he didn't want any of them to be his. In ten different timestreams, he is killed, and in six of those he's killed before he even manages to shoot anyone. In one world, the gun falls to the steps with a clatter, and he runs and doesn't stop when a cop demands that he does, and he's shot in the back. In another, he gets scared in the dark storage area and shouts at a shadow to stop moving and fires upon it and a bullet punctures a heating pipe and high-pressure steam takes off his face. In another, he gets to the loading dock, looks around at the mannequins in school uniforms being prepped for the stage, blows them to splinters and then shoots himself in the head. In yet another, he leaves the statues unmolested, but stands close to them when he puts a bullet in his brain in the hope of an artful splatter.

What's the difference between one Holbrook and the next? I'm as young as Dave, though I've lived until my late thirties in some contexts, and I have no clue. The only thing I know is that Erin trapped me here in the

Ylem, to live and relive every possibility, and they all end poorly.

Dave can't afford to practise with his Uzis. He has to get in close, keep his finger from just squeezing and freezing. Decisions are made, and with every decision a new world is born. With every decision carried out, that is.

Dave skips school again on Wednesday. He's very hungry, so he buys three cheeseburgers at the old-fashioned white-tile McDonald's close to Hamilton, and eats them by the window. *You're officially casing a joint, Mr. Holbrook*, he thinks. Or I think it to him. It's hard to tell. Mostly he has his eyes out for Erin. But she's not anywhere near school anymore. Not in that body, anyway. She's wherever chthonic goddesses go, deep underground, between manifestations. One of the two Uzis is in an oversized satchel at Dave's feet.

The Wednesday assembly involves a number of black and Latino actors and dancers in matching tracksuits. Dave's so horrified at the idea of a hip-hop breakdancing anti-bullying spectacle that he's almost upset that he's going to miss the show. When the lights dim, he slips in via the loading dock—which is kept open for fire safety reasons during assemblies—and then opens the trapdoor by what used to be the orchestra pit and heads down to the basement. The rapping is terrible, a cloying riff on "Woo Hah!! Got You All In Check" by Busta Rhymes. Something about putting bullies in check before they wreck and it's all about respec' so let's break it down on this here deck—that sort of nonsense. Admirable sentiments all around. In the basement, all Dave hears is the thumping of the bass, and his own racing heart. He's relieved to be free of the gun, but he's sweating so much that he's sure the police could find his DNA on the satchel if they were to discover this hidey-hole and locate the gun. *Which is impossible!* he reminds himself, except that it isn't impossible. Entropy decreasing is impossible. Order forming out of chaos is impossible. The destruction of energy rather than its transformation is impossible. Someone finding the Uzi before tomorrow and calling the cops, and the cops figuring out that the gun belongs to Dave is just very unlikely. Except for the *belongs to Dave* part. Who else is wandering around Hamilton with a broken nose, a broken home, and a constant hydrocodone high?

Scratch the broken nose and there were plenty of possible suspects. Dave still doesn't feel safe.

CHAPTER 21

Ann is home and ranting to herself in the master bedroom when Dave comes home from school. Her clothes are in disarray all over the floor and the unmade double bed. For a moment Dave pictures Erin straddling his father there too, naked save for little girl socks with pink ruffles, raising her hips twice a second like a machine.

"You!" Ann says to Dave. It's a blast furnace of a phoneme. Dave nearly bursts into tears and admits everything. He stole the money, the purse, has a submachine gun in his room. *Let's put one end of the hose in the exhaust and the other in the car and commit suicide instead*! But Ann is fast. "Pack a bag! We're leaving tonight!"

"What? Why?"

"Because your pedophile rapist father is coming home tonight, and if I have to see him again, I'll kill him."

"You knew . . ."

"Oh, did *you* know?" Ann drops what she's holding

and gets right up in Dave's face. She's not been drinking. Her breath smells like ash and shit instead of sweet wine. "Was that little bitch one of your classmates?"

"Uhm . . . it's a big school," Dave says. "I just mean, how did you know?"

"They were going at it in front of the window. I hollered at them, even threw a rock, but they ignored me. Your fucking father ignored me while fucking a teenager on my couch. I sit on that couch every night." She has more to say, but no more breath with which to say it. Instead she just huffs and gasps for air in front of Dave for several long seconds. "I should burn this fucking place down," she says. "Let him come home to ruins. That would be fitting, wouldn't it? But I won't. Pack a bag."

"Where are we going?" Dave says.

"A hotel. The Doubletree by the ShopRite. The motel by the Holland Tunnel, whatchamacallit? Any place but here. Good thing I don't have a gun, David. I know he's your father and you don't understand, but if I see his face, I'll kill him." She would. Dave knows the feelings. Is that where it came from, somewhere in mom's genome?

"Well, what will we do next?" Dave says. "After the hotel." *Keep her talking, Mr. Holbrook.* "We need to sit down and talk this out. Not with Dad I mean, but just—"

"David, you are a child. There's nothing to discuss."

"Well, go downstairs and think it over. I'll order pizza. Have a drink and try to relax. Then we can really think of something. Call a lawyer. I bet you could get the house in your name, or a restraining order, or something."

Ann looks skeptical. But she licks her lips. "I need to call my sister. Maybe Julia too, talk this out. But pack your bags."

"I have a test tomorrow," Dave says. "With Mr. McCann."

"So? We're not going to Egypt. Pack. A. Bag."

Dave goes to his room, unplugs the phone line from the modem, and calls his father's cell phone. It goes to voicemail, but Dave leaves a message. "Mom's superdrunk and unconscious on the couch. Please come get me." Then he tips the bureau over again, finds his emergency Robitussin and drinks half the bottle and gets into bed. His stomach roils and he cuddles his Uzi like a teddy bear, not caring if his father comes in and kicks the door to pieces. By the time Jeremy comes home to Ann, who is only half-unconscious, the screaming argument is like nothing but a half-remembered dream. It's not a good night's sleep, but it is a long night's sleep. Dave is leaving for school early in the morning, after all. He dreams of Erin and behind her, a great black thing taller and wider than his range of vision. It is black, and scaly, and writhes with dozens of coiling limbs and necks. He is Typhon, and his hundred dragon heads scrape the stars.

CHAPTER 22

Dave wakes up early to the sound of his parents fucking. They were shouting like teenagers, and the whole upper floor of the house seemed to quake with each thrust and thump.

Well, Mr. Holbrook, it's time to ruin someone's day.

Dave is hungry, and a little nauseated. He decides to keep it that way. He likes the edge, the taste of saliva and nothing else in his mouth. He doesn't have a kilt, but that'll be fine. Tigger won't be doing much complaining once he sees the gun. Oleg's a good kid. Dave will send him home.

He walks to school in the morning twilight and gets there an hour early, as planned. As usual, the metal detector hasn't even been plugged in but the doors are open for the teachers and the custodians. The security guard doesn't look up from his breakfast. Even after Columbine, nobody worries about a nerdy white kid who gets the shit kicked out of him all the time. It's getting hard to think. His mind is hazy, full of twisting black clouds.

If I see Erin, I'm going to shoot her.

I wish I had some Robitussin.

I should have brought my Gameboy to pass the time.

"Mr. Holbrook!" It's McCann.

Dave turns. Why is he here? Why is he here with an Uzi in hand, another hidden in a safe spot? Erin's guns. Of course she wouldn't be here today, and neither would his parents. Nobody to shout, "See what you made me do!" at, while pointing at a few bullet-riddled bodies. It's too late now. McCann has to be on to him. The gun's just barely hidden.

They have a brief conversation about McCann needing some help. Dave brandishes the gun. Then the world splits. In one, he doesn't shoot. In one, he does. Then the world splits again. McCann falls in both, screaming and clutching his side. In one, Dave runs right out of the school. In the other, he shoots the guard, then turns on his heel and heads deeper into the school.

A few minutes go by and a crowd gathers—students, teachers, Vice Principal Fusco. McCann's alive, the guard isn't. Sirens in the distance already. Dave opens a second-story window right over the school entrance and empties the magazine into the crowd, just in time for the cops to roll in to a generalized panic.

Hamilton's an old urban school. Lots of hallways, plenty of corners, difficult to surround. Almost nobody is inside, so that's a blessing. The JCPD uses an old playbook—circumscribe the building and wait. Dave conserves the second magazine as best he can. He's not a great shot, and the Uzi isn't a sniper rifle, so all he can do is run from one side of the building to another and occasionally plink at an ambulance, or a cop car. The door to the principal's office is locked, but he puts a few bullets through the marbled glass window on the door and manages to wing a secretary. She cries and calls for help on the phone. Her voice is an echo in Dave's mind. He loves it. *If only Erin was here.*

Dave isn't in very good shape. After thirty minutes, he's coated in sweat from all the running. He's nearly out of ammunition. He decides to head down to the basement and retrieve the second Uzi, but first he fires a single shot in the air and screams as loudly as he can. Only after does he realize that people who shoot themselves in the head probably can't scream right after, but he hopes the police will be lured in anyway.

In the dark, he has a conversation with Erin. An imaginary one.

"Happy yet?"

I'm always happy, Dave.

"Did I kill anyone outside? I guess that security guard is dead, huh?"

I think someone out there is going to die. But it might be because of a heart attack, or from falling in a dirty puddle and getting an infection in her wound.

"*Her* wound?"

You know the girls deserve it too. They're why the guys spend all their time punching your lights out. To show off. They get blowjobs and cupcakes in exchange from those bitches.

"Lucky me—you never gave me anything like that."

You wouldn't have liked my cupcakes.

"If you were here right now, I'd fucking shoot you too."

You'd try.

Nothing for a while. Then in Dave's head, Erin's voice

again. I hear too, from the Ylem. It's distinct from the imitation Dave was doing.

Well, I will give you a present now.

"What?"

There's a fuse box by the boiler room that runs the fire alarm system. Open the box, mess with the fuses, the alarm will go off. Then the cops and the fire department will have to storm the place.

Dave has nothing to say to that. He's hungry. He's bored. Running down the hallways was nothing at all like a video game, thanks to McCann and his own nervous trigger finger. He doesn't even know if he managed to nail any of his tormenters with his random bursts out the window.

So he walks to the back, pulls the alarm, and then heads back up the ladder to the trapdoor. He feels like a grunt in Vietnam, half-hidden in a foxhole. The door's heavy atop his head, and he doesn't have a great shot, but when the cops check the auditorium they likely won't see him in the pit until it's too late.

Erin's present works very well. The first SWAT guy to enter the auditorium gets his ankles chewed off, and the room's too large to gas effectively. Dave gets to empty a whole magazine into the bulletproof vests, replace it, fire off a few more shots, then drop back down into the basement, throw the gun away, and wait on his belly with his arms behind his back for his arrest. Shooting cops is much cooler than shooting kids, he decides. It's not like these cops will shoot him in cold blood. Not until he's a grown up.

The Uzi is recovered with ten bullets still in the clip. From prison Dave explains that those ten bullets belong to the world now. Ten bullets for the picked-on kids, for the oppressed peoples across the planet, to deliver as they see fit into the heads of their tormentors. *Does not the schematic symbol for resistor have ten points?* The esoteric meaning is so clear it's actually exoteric. When selling antinomianism to high schoolers, the Kallis Episkipos had to keep things simple.

O

Then there's the world where Dave ran. The gun was like a snake in his hand—terrifying, dangerous, and strangely compelling all the same. He couldn't drop the gun and surrender, but hearing McCann howl like an animal, seeing the fat security guard switch off like an old machine, drained the fluid from Dave's spine. He bolted back down the steps, Uzi in hand. He smelled like hell.

Officer Ford is on the corner. He spots the gun and bellows for Dave to stop. Dave points the Uzi and says, "No, you! I mean . . ." Then he turns and runs. His fingers feel huge, the gun so small. He couldn't pull the trigger if he wanted to. He wants to throw the gun away, but there's no turning back. There's still a small rational part of him saying, *You can't go back home. You can't go anywhere. All you have is that gun. You can trade it. You can sell it. You can use it to get out of here. Don't worry, you won't have to shoot anyone else.*

That small rational part of him was me. I often wonder if Erin put me here in the Ylem just for this reason— to keep David alive beyond the end of the day. Once he entered the school with the gun, a near-infinity of alternative lives ended, like a tree being pruned of almost all its branches. I could guide him away from putting the gun to his own head, from turning the wrong corner and being gunned down by the police.

Erin's house!

Let the cops find him there. Either she's home and is just a semi-messed up girl, and it doesn't matter; or she's not home and it doesn't matter; or she is Eris the goddess of discord and can deal with a SWAT team blowing away her pig-fat golem of a father and sending a wall of bullets right at her, then she raises her palm and the bullets stop mid-air and fall to the ground like it's bullettime for real, and then everything matters.

Sirens are already everywhere, and Dave's lungs feel like they're full of hot coals. He zig-zags his way through the crowds on the streets, his borrowed coat flapping like broken bat wings. A familiar car roars his way. He thinks it's Jeremy's at first and is ready to empty a clip into the windshield, but this is an older, dumpier Nissan, and it jumps the curb right in front of him.

Uncle Bill sticks his head out the driver's side window. "Get in!" he shouts. Dave makes a grab for the back door and throws himself onto the seat. The car takes off before he can slam the door shut behind him, and he nearly gets the edge of the duster caught, but he finally closes it.

Uncle Bill takes a portable blue light from the seat next to him, puts it on the dash, and clicks it on.

"Holy shit, you're a cop!" Dave trembles hard, vomits a little. I scream at every one of his nerve endings *Don't shoot*! and he manages not to.

"I *was* a cop. Then I got mixed up with a little bitch of our mutual acquaintance," Uncle Bill says. "Ended up working for her papa in the restaurant, just to be near her. Then they moved to Jersey, and I didn't get to see her nearly as much." He looks old and worn out now—a young face, but his skin is a little ashy, there are wrinkles around his eyes, and his black hair is splattered with grey. "Sorry about the stabbing. I did it for her."

"She told you to stab me . . ."

"Naw," he says. "I just did it because I had the feeling she wanted me to."

"Where are you taking me?"

"First, out of Hudson County. Then out of New Jersey."

"Are we going to meet her somewhere? In the city?"

Uncle Bill just laughs and laughs.

The siren makes the traffic part, renders traffic lights irrelevant, and even lets Dave zip by real police cars. But there's no radio in the car, no barrier between front seat and back, nor any of the other stuff he expects to see even in an undercover cop car. Uncle Bill is silent, his eyes slits as he drives.

They get on the turnpike, and the light isn't enough. Bill clicks a button and a siren starts, but it sounds like it's coming from the car radio speakers, and doesn't quite match the siren sounds Dave has heard before. Regardless, the cars part like the Red Sea and the Nissan blows past commuters by the dozen.

"Where are we going? Pennsylvania?" *Too far*. Dave knows nobody down there, doesn't even know where the good neighbourhoods and the bad ones are. In the distance, the Meadowlands. Dave knows it. Uncle Bill's police stunt has cleared the traffic on both sides of the vehicle. In the air, a helicopter swoops in. News or police, Dave can't tell.

Do it! I tell him, and amazingly, he does. He opens the door and throws himself out. Adrenaline takes over. Even in the Ylem, I'm as drunk with it as he is. He doesn't feel the wound on his side re-opening, or the tooth loosening when he hits the asphalt. He's back up, gun out to ward off traffic in five stumbling steps, and he runs for the guardrail. Uncle Bill's Nissan screeches as it fishtails. Dave hops the guardrail and hits the grass hard.

On your belly! I tell him. *Crawl!* One of us had some military training—National Guard when Jeremy refused to pay for college, and what one Dave Holbrook knows, I know, and I told Dave the routine: *I'm up! He sees me! I'm down!* Uncle Bill drove up to the railing, got out of the car, and vaulted over the rail. We were extremely lucky. He had his hazard lights on—still putting on the cop act—and left his keys in the ignition. Dave wanted to take a shot, but it was hard enough to crawl in the muck, to push forward on elbows and knees, hard to breathe in the shit. He almost passed out, but managed to loop around while Bill searched the underbrush. Another burst of speed was all he needed to get into the car and lock himself in.

Dave had some small experience behind the wheel— no driver's ed class, but a few spins around the parking lot and one harrowing night when Ann made him take the PATH to Hoboken and drive her back home from a bar—but I had a lot more. I pushed as hard as I could from the femtosecond in front of him. He got the car in reverse and slammed on the accelerator. The light afternoon traffic gave Dave a wide berth.

Dave had never been to Kearny, but I knew something about it. As an adult—as the man who'd brandished his gun at Mr. McCann but *did not shoot*—I'd been there once

on an abortive third date. Third dates are dealmakers
or dealbreakers. Either you get laid or get laid off. The
woman, her name was Louise and we'd met at work,
revealed the existence of her five-year-old son by way
of introducing him. Cute kid, looked more like his white
father than his black mother. His name was Louie, named
for his mother. And we went to a local carnival. It was a
typical Jersey night—hot and sticky and swarming with
mosquitoes. Kearny is just twelve miles from Manhattan,
and about one hundred years away.

We were walking down the midway, mostly pulling the
boy past the crooked games and other joints the charms
to which long hours and low wages at the state lottery
commission had immunized us, when a barker outside
the dark ride called Summer Tentacular started to tell a
joke into a megaphone.

"Hey, I got a funny story for you all! This nigger walks
into a bar—" Louise's head snapped to. "Oh! There's
one here!" he blurted out. The boy started to cry. Louise
picked him up and started walking back toward the
parking lot. A few people dared jeer and call out to her,
"Hey, it's just a joke! What's *your* problem!" Her face was
stone. We didn't kiss goodnight. I didn't know what to
say except "Sorry" and she wasn't interested in even
that. "Did you know that this fucking town," she told me
as she put Louie in his car seat over his wiggling, wailing,
protests, "is named after a Civil War general?"

So yes, Kearny would do. We found the exit quickly
enough and drove through Harrison, which I remembered
well, right into the centre of town. Then we abandoned
the car, parking it in front of the pork store from *The
Sopranos*. Kearny is all squat little brick buildings, and

the occasional public monolith—a small town that once had hopes to be a bigger one.

The high school wasn't far, and it had recently been let out, probably thanks to reports of a shooting in Jersey City. Dave heads there for no other reason than school is familiar. If he has a plan at all, it belongs to me, and if I have a plan at all, it's because I've seen this particular strand of life—including my own ghostly role in it—play out over and over. Do you root for Luke Skywalker when you watch *Star Wars*? So do I, even though the scenes of his defeat, and victory, have already been shot, edited, developed, printed, scanned, uploaded, and digitally toyed with a dozen times.

There's a peculiar sociological inevitability when it comes to schooling in New Jersey, where the rich snobs and the street kids and poor immigrants and fourth-generation Princeton legacies still occasionally find themselves sentenced to nine hours a day in the same prison. But it's the ones least prepared for school who stick around. Rich kids have their lessons and hobbies and PlayStations; ambitious ones go home and get their homework done, or work for their parents in a little store. The kids who are nothing but trouble in school, they have nothing to do but mill around the bleachers, the handball court, the parking lot when it lets out early.

Oleg's coat is in tatters, so Dave just uses it as gift-wrapping for the gun. He removes the magazine and drops it into a mailbox about a block from the school, then he finds a likely crowd.

There's a quartet of excitable kids with pasty Irish faces milling around the school. They see Dave and their conversation stops. He's a sight—nose still bandaged, new bruises and swamp mud all over his pants, and he's carrying what probably looks like a dead animal from a distance. If he were an adult, the kids would probably just assume that Dave was homeless and crazy. Their parents would call the police, or seriously contemplate moving. Kearny is where one goes to get away from the scum of Newark and Jersey City.

Dave is beyond caring. He can talk to people, finally. Face the day without cough syrup, for now. He needs money and knows of two ways to get it. Along this branch of time, he chooses the safer way.

"Hey, guys," he says, his voice dry and squeaky. "Wanna see something cool—that's for sale?" He looks over his left shoulder, then right, and then unwraps the Uzi.

The guys are stunned. Dave is surprised too, when the smallest of the quartet steps up to speak. "What the fuck?" says the kid, who looks like someone carefully put a T-shirt on a mailbox.

"It's real."

"You want us to buy a machine gun from a stranger?" the kid says.

"You don't want one?"

"What the fuck would we do with it?" one of the other guys says. He's a tall one, and he speaks slowly like every word is invented just before it's enunciated.

Dave just shrugs. He turns the gun's barrel toward himself, offering the grip.

"You're the kid from Newark who just killed everyone at his school, aren't you? How the hell did you get out to Kearny?" the lead kid says. The others have gone from surprised to simmering, sneaking half steps around Dave, flanking him.

"Magic," Dave says. "Don't worry guys, the gun isn't loaded. See, no magazine." And he pulls the trigger. Nothing, but the kids jump back. "See, nothing," Dave says.

"Then we can take the gun from you," the lead kid says.

"You can try." There's steel in Dave's voice now. "Better men than you lot have tried to fuck with me. Guess what happened to them?" The Kearny kids could guess, but I knew—nothing.

"I want that gun," one of the kids says. He had been silent till now. His eyes met Dave's, and Dave knew. This kid, with his shock of red hair and weird tooth and awkward limbs and slightly older clothes, had to be somebody's cousin. He wouldn't have been tolerated otherwise. They would have chewed him up in middle school and left him ruined and alone. "How much?" He licks his lips when he talks.

"I'm a motivated seller," Dave says. Indeed, he's half-ready to just hand over the Uzi and run. But he needs money to live. There's a new life ahead of him—a life on the streets, of sleeping in garbage bins, of keeping an eye out for the cops, of pissing and shitting in alleyways and on street corners. He can't wait to start, actually. "How much do you guys have?"

The tall slow guy opens his mouth again, like he's inventing language. "But . . . this is an escalation. We got a gun, then what will happen if the Avenue Boys find out?"

"How many times a week do you think someone's

going to show up in town offering an Uzi for cheap?"
the lead kid says. "They ain't gonna get a gun like this.
Tommy's right. Let's buy it. Turn out your pockets,
dudes." Together the kids have seventy bucks—the one
who never said a word coughed up two twenty-dollar
bills on his own. Dave hands the gun to the red-haired
Tommy, tells them where the clip is, and the trade is
made. Somewhere in his mind he giggles and thinks, *A
Tommy gun for Tommy!* He takes off before being roped
into an argument about where the gang is going to keep
their gun, and how best to get the magazine out of the
mailbox. That's the thing about even numbers: lots of tie
votes.

Dave thinks he's one, but he's really two, and I'm really
many. There won't be a tie vote with us anymore. *Mr.
Holbrook!* I tell him. *Get out of this city.* Kearny is too small
for a strange runaway with no connections to anyone in
town, with no friends. I'm getting better, maybe thanks
to the fact that Dave's own mind is shutting down. All
it can conceive of is a great red spot spreading over the
guard's belly, a tiny gurgling noise, the smell of metal
and fire.

He heads over to a drugstore and buys a cheap hoodie,
some Robitussin, and two small packages of Hostess
Cupcakes. Calories and sugar is what he needed now. He
tries out his Spanish on the cashier—*En dónde está la
parada de autobús?*—and she answers at a fast clip Dave
can't understand. He shrugs and says, "Any English," and
she says, "You can get the cheap bus to the city one block
down." That's what he wanted. The official NJ Transit
buses are probably under surveillance. The semi-illicit
minibuses that bring maids and manual workers to and

from the city for a dollar or two were safer. Dave, with his filthy clothing and crumpled paper bag and chocolate on his lips, would stand out, but his fellow passengers were less likely to talk about it. That's what Dave hopes anyway.

The bus comes quickly enough, and the driver collects Dave's two dollars without looking up. Dave is sick to his stomach again. He wishes he had a radio, or at least that there would be a breaking news announcement on the station the bus driver is listening to. It would have to be about him, if there was one. *Right?*

Maybe, I tell him, playing the executive function. *Just take it easy. Put your hood up.*

The Meadowlands come into view, then Secaucus and Weehawken, which looks just like Jersey City except that Dave doesn't recognize any of the buildings. There are cop cars at the Lincoln Tunnel, but aren't there always, since 9/11? Dave tries to remember if there were any cameras in the hallways back at Hamilton. It hardly matters—there are roll calls and Delaney Cards, and two parents back at home ready to blabber about months of awkward behaviour and lone-wolfisms. There's a plastic bag in the bedroom closet full of sticky empties from his cough syrup habit. He even wore a long coat to school. His computer has Limewire, and he's downloaded not only songs, but porn from the Internet. It's all on his hard drive.

Dave pukes into the paper bag on his lap, earning a glare from an older man two rows ahead of him. The bus slows as it curves around the long road to the Lincoln Tunnel and reaches the bottleneck at its mouth. A cop walks between lanes, but not purposefully. I tell Dave to look away but he can't help but stare as the cop walks by. The cop stares back, but doesn't raise an eyebrow or point or reach for his walkie-talkie. Dave wishes that the cop reached for his gun and put a bullet in his head. The big red bloom on his mind again, this time erupting out of his own skull, like cough syrup splattered against a bathroom wall.

Dave makes it to the Port Authority. The buses are expensive. Everything is expensive in New York. Four dollars for a cup of soup at a restaurant, three bucks for a slice of pizza. He thinks about choosing some random chock-full-of-snore town: Wilkes-Barre, Pennsylvania, or Danbury, Connecticut, and just vanishing, but it's thirty or forty bucks. He has only sixty to last him. The McDonald's dollar menu and the twenty-four hour toilets will be better bets for him. He could last a month out here in the city, and that's if he never makes another dime.

We have a plan. Downtown, the Barnes & Noble stores on 23rd Street and Union Square. That's the day shift. Read books, listen to music, check the couches for loose change, the trash bins by the Starbucks for scraps. Wash up in the restrooms. Night shift, St. Mark's Place. Where the crusty punks hang out. Make some friends. Do some begging. Maybe find a dreadlocked girl with a pet pit bull who likes her guys skinny and smelly and tasting like synthetic grapes. Make friends. Sleep on couches if possible, in doorways if not. It's unanimous. We have chosen to stay and fight.

enough to trace back to a certain employee at Washington Place Diner and Restaurant.

After a cold week on the streets, after nearly being arrested for sleeping at Barnes & Noble, after five days of literally not uttering a word to anyone, Dave tries the diner. Erin isn't there. Uncle Bill isn't there. Mr. Zevgolis is. He'd just rung up someone's bill—twenty-three dollars—on the old analog cash register. Dave walks in, ignores the sign reading PLEASE WAIT TO BE SEATED and hops onto the stool right next to the register, in front of a dirty plate. Zevgolis eyes him. Dave takes a crescent-shaped bit of silver dollar pancake from the plate, takes a second to admire the jagged bite mark on its interior curve, and then puts it in his mouth. Killing someone changes you. We're all different now, except for the Dave Holbrooks in cosmically parallel Middlesex County Juvenile Detention Centers—they're the ones who never took their shot.

"No homeless," Zevgolis says, and for a moment Dave doesn't even realize that the man's talking about him.

Dave doesn't bother looking at his own reflection in the napkin holder, or in the mirror behind the soda machine. Instead he just says, "Yes homeless," and scoops up some remnant syrup with two fingers, then sucks them clean. Zevgolis snatches the plate away and barks a command in Greek. A girl comes out. She's young, plain, with dark hair and dead eyes. She takes the plate and hustles it to the back. She looks quite a bit like Erin, but not quite. A cousin. Maybe even a sister.

"Where's Erin?" Dave asks.

"None of your business," Zevgolis says. "I call the police."

CHAPTER 23

What is it about the number twenty-three? Nothing, really. It's just that most world events are directly tied in with the number somehow. That was in a book I read once—one Tigger had pushed into my hands in school and said I just had to read. The enigma of twenty-three is well-known enough that Hollywood even made a shitty movie about it a few years after Dave fired his Uzi and ran.

Four years on the street was hard for Dave. He lost a tooth the hard way. East Village street life, as it turns out, wasn't full of clever punk rock girls who delight in sucking off unshowered boys from New Jersey. Dave was on the news quite a bit, for a while. His awkward school ID photo loomed large in the public consciousness for nearly two months. None of the journalists, none of the reporters, ever made any mention of Erin, though she did spring him from the hospital, didn't she? Though the second Uzi was eventually found in Hamilton High School's basement, and that should have been easy

BULLETTIME

"Okay," Dave says. "Call. You think they won't want to talk to her when I start talking to them?"

"No police," Zevgolis says. He leaves the register and walks down the length of the counter, and says something in Greek to the short-order cook at the pick-up window. Then he's handed a cleaver and casually strolls back toward where Dave is sitting. "No police!" he says again, raising the cleaver. "Fine!" Dave scrambles off the stool and, hands up, runs backward out of the restaurant.

He spends a lot of time milling around the West Village after that, hoping to get a glimpse of Erin coming to or leaving from the restaurant. He doesn't get one. That other girl, that strange and dim photocopy of Erin, yes, all the time. He dares not take the PATH train back to Jersey City, even after autumn turns to winter and his name falls from the pages of the newspapers he uses as blankets every night. The Jefferson Library is nearby, picturesque and quiet. Dave does his research, and even manages to get a library card by stealing someone's electric bill from an apartment building vestibule and spending a few of his precious dollars on an unofficial ID for the name on the bill. Then he gets online for the first time in months.

Dave has fans. Not so many as he would have had he killed more people, surrendered to the police, ranted and drooled purple slobber in front of the TV cameras, but he has fans. People who find his actions understandable, who list some of the problems he had in bullet points, who write stories about him invading Hogwarts and killing all the Slytherin. Between fan websites, LiveJournal communities, and bulletin boards—two are dedicated to trying to "find" him, one features a photo of his head

Photoshopped atop the body of a machine-gun wielding terrorist in all black—he has twenty-three different fan groups.

He knows not to check his own email. He's so hungry that he creates a new Yahoo! email address and begins to type up a message demanding money, or food, from the people trafficking in his name. But he can't prove himself to these people, and some of them might be cops. His ID is under a fake name, and even if he managed to set up a PayPal account, what could he do with it except slosh the money around the Internet? Send himself a fruit basket. Sign up to Cookie of the Month club and loiter around the vestibule of the address on his ID on delivery day.

Except … one of his fans is local. She lives in the Village. She's in grad school at NYU, studying microcelebrity and camgirls. She does performance art and neoburlesque. Sometimes. Not that Dave can afford a seven-dollar cover charge, not that his fake ID or library card would pass muster at a door even on Ludlow Street. But this woman, her name is Anne B., is having a show on the, yes, twenty-third. *Bullettime*. Starts at 11 p.m., which is the twenty-third hour of the day. Not on 23rd Street, of course—no downtown kid ever crosses 14th Street, unless he or she is a secret trustafarian.

Dave's attention shifts toward Washington Square Park and the NYU buildings that surround it. New York's a populous city, NYU a large school, but there are patterns in all our lives, and the Village is still a neighbourhood. The rasta drug dealers and the Jesus Easel guy may as well clock in and out for all their regularity. Dave has a print-out of Anne B. in his pocket, and with every orbit of the park, past the dogs and the chess players and the skateboarders and the flocks of pigeons who roar up from the earth and then settle back down, Dave feels a sense of destiny. But Anne B. never walks through the park, or appears in the little public lounge on the first floor of the Bobst Library, or even comes into the student centre. Someone else hangs her flyers for her. He also hangs flyers for freelance term-paper writers, NYPIRG, and B'nai B'rith International, so Anne probably just paid a service.

When it snows, it's actually warmer. The wind isn't so frigid, the sidewalks are more welcoming. Dave finds a decent vent to sleep near for one, and has the night to himself without even a moment's molestation by police, shopkeepers, or rival homeless. He's glad he's young, that he doesn't have to shave too often to keep looking civilized. He can go to Forbidden Planet and skim the comics without being ejected, bring soda cans into the supermarket and get back a handful of nickels without being sent outside to get in line behind the bums and their filled-to-bursting shopping carts. He's clean enough to occasionally turn to someone and ask for a quarter, or a dollar—and get it, and it doesn't even seem like begging. Just borrowing. When he goes to shoplift, he hits the local mom and pop pharmacies for cough syrup and soap, because they're less likely to have surveillance cameras and fascist mandatory prosecution policies. The soap is important. He can stay clean enough to pass by washing up in a sink—plenty of hipsters and street kids are a little rank. He has three shirts and two pairs of jeans. The clothes not on his back are carefully hidden in the Jefferson Library branch. If he can stay on the right side of the line, Dave can live an almost normal life out on the streets.

Most of all, Dave misses pasta, which you can't buy from a cart and rarely find clean in a Dumpster. Brute survival, and his fan Anne B., push the red bloom of the security guard's stomach out of his dreams. There's one day when Dave doesn't even think about Erin until almost four o'clock, when he walks by a school letting out. But Erin is always on my mind.

Dave still thinks of me as nothing but the voice of his own self-talk, but I smile when I see the club—it's called Collective: Unconscious—and he smiles too. He just doesn't know why. Dave was mistaken; it's not a bar or the sort of club one needs ID to get into. No drinking, no Ticketmaster. The place is just an old storefront with the counters and cash registers torn out and some folding chairs put in. The woman at the door, a meaty girl with fire-engine-red hair and tattoo sleeves, wants seven dollars. Dave only has five, and he looks so skinny and pathetic and his stomach is growling audibly even as he negotiates. The woman takes the money and waves him in.

Dave expects to have to force his way to the front, but the place is practically empty. Most of the folding chairs are still neatly stacked against a far wall. A quick count—by me, not Dave—confirms that yes, there are twenty-three chairs positioned before what passes for a stage. Dave has his pick; he's early, and the first one here. Collective: Unconscious smells vaguely of Chinese food, and so Dave's stomach rumbles even more loudly.

He can't bring himself to sit in the front row, so chooses the second, but right in the middle.

Already he's nervous. Burning up. Life outside changes a person. Any room smaller than a subway station feels claustrophobic, and the air smells old and sick—full of disease. Dave's throat tickles, and though he had shoplifted some cough syrup the other day, he is afraid to pull it from the pocket of his soiled hoodie and take a swig. Even though he's clearing his throat time and again, even though he might really be a little sick, and there's nobody to challenge him.

The audience enters in twos and threes. Dave is very used to being alone. It's how I've managed to get and stay so close to him. Forget that poor state worker who rarely had conversations with more than one person at a time, Dave hasn't said more than ten words to anyone since Mr. Zevgolis, and that was months ago. But we can chat sometimes. Someone came in with a slice of pizza. Dave's mouth fills with saliva. He's dizzy with rage, ready to just grab the pizza, shove it in his mouth, and run. But the lights dim and he relaxes.

There's no introduction, no plea for funds, no welcome. Anne B. appears from a door that once led to a storeroom and steps onto the stage. She's attractive, a little older than her publicity photo or website pics. He can see her crow's feet, the bulge of her underarms atop the black leather corset she's wearing. The white nurse stockings don't match. She opens her mouth and screeches. *So this is performance art, Mr. Holbrook,* Dave thinks. He drinks his cough syrup. Nobody's paying attention to him.

Collective: Unconscious doesn't have a complex

lighting rig, but it's enough for the show. Anne B.'s on-stage authority is cut to ribbons by streaks of light over shadow. She starts chanting in a language Dave does not know. Her palms are up, then vanish into the dark. She turns her head, and from a speaker hidden somewhere in the room a distant-seeming horn sounds.

Dave looks around, trying to catch the eye of the other audience members, but they're all rapt and peering up at the stage. The lights shift again, to red and blue. Anne B. starts telling a story about a time her boyfriend convinced her to wear a buttplug. Not just at home, in bed, but out and about. They went to Kings Plaza, in Brooklyn, and ate at the food court.

"'Get it yet, slut?' he said," she says.

"'I do, Sir,' I said, not caring who might hear me call him Sir."

"'Oh yah? What do you get?'" she says, modulating her voice. Then back to her normal voice: "'I can't stop thinking about it,' I tell him. 'Whenever I see someone sitting down a little tenderly, or working behind a counter, or walking slowly, I . . .'"

Anne B. waits a moment, and in the affected voice of the boyfriend of the story, says, "'Go on.'"

"'I just think of them all wearing plugs. Everyone's a dirty little whore wearing an assplug for their masters. The whole town is sex. I lick my lips at the thought of how wonderfully hard I'm going to get fucked tonight,'" she says. In the back of the room, someone starts applauding, but then quickly stops.

Something both sweet and sour rises up in Dave's gullet. He thinks of his mother, what she would say if she were here now. Probably something like, *Yup, that's performance art for you. It's always the same. I used to . . .* and then like the thought itself, she would trail off. It's getting hotter in the room—Dave drank his cough syrup too quickly, and he can't keep it down.

"Let's you and I," Anne B. says as she takes a step forward into a new light with a weird multicoloured gel, "form a secret society. Just the twenty-three of us." There's a man in the far corner with an old-fashioned overhead projector fresh from a high school somewhere, and some coloured liquid to draw bloblike shapes all over her limbs and face. "Tell no one."

Dave opens his mouth and the cough syrup comes pouring out. The second spasm of vomit is even louder. Nobody's clapping now, but indeed nobody is responding. Is this just all part of the show? Anne B. doesn't miss a beat. "That's right! Let it all out, baby!" she says, and Dave vomits again.

"No, you don't understand!" Dave shouts. "This is real! I'm homeless! I don't have access to a washer and dryer. I have two fucking outfits. I need help! I—" There's more, but there's also still more cough syrup in Dave's gullet, and it comes up.

"C'mon, get him out of here," someone says, and the house lights go on, but with a stomp of her foot and a bellowed *"Don't you dare!"* from Anne B. the house lights go back off and the phantasmagorical spotlight on. Anne B. produces a ukulele and starts strumming. Dave has nothing to lose. He wishes he had his Uzi—that would let him teach this asinine crowd some lessons. He rushes the stage. Anne screams and tries to ward him off with her ukulele. Then he's rushed by the large woman who was at the door, who wraps her arms around him.

"This isn't part of the show!" she yells. "Call 911!"

"Don't," Dave says. His clothing is slick enough from his own puke that he snakes out of the woman's grasp. He stumbles to the lip of the low stage, hits his shin and splays across it. Anne B. plants a foot on the small of Dave's back and finishes her song. Only on the last verse does he realize that the song is actually about him. He gives up, as does the woman who tried to restrain him, and just waits under Anne B.'s heel. The show goes on for a little bit longer, and Anne is careful to make sure that one foot always stays on Dave's back as she moves about the tiny stage. I have a sense that some latent choreography is being carried out—that the performance would have been more physically intense if not for Anne B.'s quick integration of Dave into the show. But the stage was quite small—a couple of pallets placed side by side and covered in black felt.

Soon enough it's over, but Anne B. doesn't retreat from the stage. There is no applause, just the sound of people getting their coats. The ticket-taker, who had managed only to smear Dave's puke all over her dress in an attempt to clean it off, stands in front of the stage and reads from the calendar of forthcoming events to the backs of the audience as they file out. Then she whips her head around and says, "Annie, I'm going to call the fucking cops on you, if you ever pull that shit again! Clean him up and get him out." She walks off, as though on cue in a theatrical performance that exists only in her head.

Dave looks up at Anne B. as best he can from his position on the stage, and says, "Do you know who I am?"

"Oh, honey," Anne B. says, "don't you know never to

pull any of that 'do you know who I am' crap downtown? We'll eat you alive. I will, anyway." Then she says, "Come on, Mr. Holbrook. You stink."

She leads him to a small apartment on Rivington Street, the kind with a bathtub in the living room/ kitchen. Behind the tub is a small space for a futon and beyond that is a tiny water closet. Dave's not very tall, but when he sits on the commode his knees touch the bottom of the sink. Anne hands him a pair of plastic shopping bags from the Food Lion and tells him to put his clothes in there.

"Get in the bath," she says. "You smell terrible. I had to open the window, and it's January. I have some pasta."

"Uhm . . ."

"What? There's a shower curtain."

"You'll still be able to see me," he says. "My shadow."

Anne smiles a tight little smile. "You're a poet. I promise I'll turn around and just slave away over the hot stove like your mother used to. Or you can just go back to wherever you came from, Mr. Homeless."

Dave frowns and takes the bags and steps into the bath fully clothed. It's a small tub, like everything else in the tiny studio apartment, so Dave awkwardly peels out of his clothes, shoves them into the bags, and drops them beyond the flimsy curtain. He can see Anne B.'s silhouette puttering around by the oven and the few shelves above that make up her pantry and is sure that she can see him, so he covers his genitals with one boney forearm and crouches as he turns on the faucet. He glances up—Anne is looking at him. She's sautéing onions and peering right at him instead of the saucepan. His stomach turns again, but he manages to suppress it.

Anne B. has a boy T-shirt for him, and a pair of boxer shorts, and some guy's abandoned jeans that are too big for him. *How does someone manage to walk out of a girl's apartment and leave his jeans behind*, Dave wonders. But he does not ask. Anne B. had even wiped down Dave's shoes, but threw out the socks, which were beyond saving.

They eat in silence, sitting opposite one another on a thin rug on the floor, for the most part. Laps full of food. It's hard for Dave not to just grab the noodles and shove them into his mouth. If only Anne B. had some butter—his mom used to make it with butter, not oil and onion and lentils. Only then does Dave realize that this woman and his mother share a name, that "Anne B." even sounds like a replacement model or second-generation derivative of the original Ann.

"I suppose you're waiting for me to ask something like, 'What's it like to kill a man,' and then maybe offer to suck your cock?" Anne B. says. Dave shudders so severely just from being spoken to that Anne says, "Or not! Christ, nevermind. Geez, eat." She reaches over to the mini-fridge, opens it, and hands him a can of Pabst Blue Ribbon. "Here. It's all I have. You're underage, but you're already leading a life of crime. As am I now, just for having you here."

"Is there a reward for me?" Dave says.

"Five grand."

Dave has nothing to say to that.

"It's pretty small, as far as these rewards go, really. I guess they don't have a big tax pool in Jersey. And it's not like your parents had much to say. That's why I got interested in you. You were like a media fucking darling for two seconds, but your parents just up and disappeared."

"Well, their marriage was . . ."

Anne B. raises an eyebrow. "Their son brought a machine gun to school for no reason. I'm sure their marriage was . . ."

"It wasn't like that."

"It's amazing you're alive," Anne says. "They reported all the injuries you had in the weeks leading up to the shooting attempt. Any of them could have gone septic out in the streets."

"Just lucky, I guess," Dave says. He laughs before Anne B. can. The beer isn't good, exactly, and it reminds him more of the street than anything else, but he drinks deeply from it. "It wasn't about my parents, not really. It was about a girl . . ."

Dave, in fits and starts, in between bites of pasta—he's bypassed his empty plate now and is eating right out of the pot in the middle of the floor—tells what he thinks the story is. I'm left out entirely, as are all the rest of us, all the wanderers on the roads not taken. Not that he'd know a thing about us, except for a glimpse in a hydrocodone haze.

"That's interesting that you saw a girl who looked kind of like the girl you were into, working in the same place and interacting with the same father. Sure it wasn't the same girl?"

"Yeah, of course," Dave says. "I'm not crazy or something. I mean, it could have been her, but it was like something was missing."

"What was missing? Her attention turned to you?"

"Something . . ." Dave searches for the word for a

moment, and finds it, thanks to an afternoon spent at St. Mark's Bookstore a few days prior. "Ineffable."

"Would you say," Anne says as she leans forward, over the plates, "that I have a certain ineffable something?" She flashes a little bit of cleavage; a scattering of freckles make it look almost accessible.

"You're . . ."

"Huh?"

"Her?"

"What?"

"I'm sorry, I'm sorry," Dave says. "I just thought you were trying to say something. I mean, you know things. Your show tonight—secret society?"

"Yeah, that's a good line," Anne B. says. "If I do say so myself."

"She said that," Dave says.

"I must have read that somewhere," Anne B. says. "I have a little scrapbook of you."

"Why?"

Anne B. shrugs. "What a strange question. I mean, it's a good question, but it's strange that you ask it. If someone liked, I dunno, Bruce Springsteen, do you think he'd ask 'Why?'"

"He's a musician. He tries to get your attention."

"And you weren't doing that? If not my attention . . . then that girl's?"

Dave says, "Well, it didn't work. And I ended someone's life. I think about that every day. It wasn't even anyone who had hurt me. Those assholes are still walking free." Then he realizes something. "Wait—Erin said that thing about a secret society to me, in my room. I didn't tell anyone. I didn't blog about it. There was nowhere for you to read it!"

Anne B. stands up, palms out. Her voice is slow now—she's a real actress—and soft too. "Well, let me show you my scrapbook. I'm sure I clipped some article that mentioned it."

"You know her." His voice is hard all of the sudden. The months on the street, the growling stomach, the cold that never leaves the bones, the running from the police, the crusty jeans full of piss, all in three little words. There's the killer, back again.

Anne B. doesn't answer. She does bend over to rummage through a milk crate. Even that pose is provocative, or maybe I'm just a femtosecond too close to Dave Holbrook, and not a femtosecond too far after all.

"You're from around here. Maybe you eat at the diner. You heard her talking, or she just sat down one day and told you everything. She has that way about her." Dave takes a step forward. "Where is she? Did her father send her away? Did she kill herself? You even act like her!"

Anne B. turns around, back straight. She has the receiver to a cordless phone in her hand, her finger on 1. I presume she already pressed 9, and maybe even 9 and 1. "You know, Dave, I wanted to help you out. You've been important to my work, and obviously you're sick. Maybe you shouldn't blame some girl for your problems. It's the easiest thing to leave when someone comes up with a great idea to shoot up a school, and even easier to call the police when she . . . or if she actually feels dangerous."

"It's more than that," Dave says. "All sorts of things happened. She's like a force of nature—"

"She's a kid. A kid your age," Anne B. says.

"And look at me! Hell, you wrote a song about me!" Dave Holbrook doesn't quite know, but he knows enough. He must feel me next to him, feel all of us who have had a glimpse of the Ylem. He starts babbling about Erin. Who she *really* is. The number twenty-three. "Look, even as we speak, it's two-thirty a.m.! There's a twenty-three right there. I've been noticing them everywhere, and that comes from—"

Anne B. presses 1. "Should I press it again?"

"Look," he says. No, he doesn't say it. I say it. Dave sees the phone in her hand, hears her voice in his ears, and he runs away into somewhere deep in his head. Anyone else would be catatonic, but there's me, just out of phase thanks to Eris, and so I step in. "I can prove it." I'm not supposed to do this. I've seen this film before. Anne B. makes to call the cops, Dave passes out. She has a change of heart and puts him in her bed with the help of a neighbour. He stays for two nights and three days—23!—and Anne B. even puts Dave's underage murderous cock in her mouth one night after she comes home drunk from another performance of her show. Then he leaves again, with sixty dollars in his pocket and permission to use the shower again if he has to, an offer which he never takes Anne B. up on.

But I'm in the body again, after so many months/years/decades. I can rewrite the script. "I can prove it." And I walk to the window Anne B. has left open a crack. A few desultory snowflakes drift in from outside. I throw the window open, and step out onto the fire escape. Anne B. shouts at me to come back in her best drama class Nurse Ratched voice. She can really project, but this is the Lower East Side and nobody here has cared about a screaming woman for a long, long time. It's nice to have a body again, even one half-starved and frozen and drunk. I put my hands on the railing and it's so cold it burns. I get a foot up, then the others and I feel Anne clambering out behind us. "You shouldn't be out there! Don't do it!"

It's true. I should be on the floor of the apartment, unconscious. Anne should be screaming, but different words. The river of time has already been dammed up. This is a strange new universe—one where we can write our own destinies. One where I can, anyway. I can do anything now. "I shouldn't be anywhere!" I tell Anne. I don't turn back to look at her though, so maybe she doesn't know I'm smiling. "And I can do whatever I like." I take a step and show her what I mean by walking across the nothing, two stories over the asphalt. Then I cross the street and turn down the block, heading west toward the river, and New Jersey.

END

ACKNOWLEDGEMENTS

This book was a long and weird time coming. For a few years there, it seemed that whenever a publishing company got interested in *Bullettime*, there would be a school shooting and I'd receive a rejection letter. So thanks, in the first instance, to ChiZine Publications for being less skittish, and luckier. I'd also like to thank Carrie Laben and Tim Pratt for enthusiastic early reads, and Olivia Flint for more or less everything, as always.

ABOUT THE AUTHOR

Nick Mamatas is the author of four and a half previous novels, including *The Damned Highway* with Brian Keene, and *Sensation*. He's also an anthologist—recent titles include *Haunted Legends*, co-edited with Ellen Datlow, and *The Future is Japanese*, co-edited with Masumi Washington. Nick's short fiction has appeared in *Asimov's Science Fiction*, *Weird Tales*, *New Haven Review*, and the Canadian literary journal *subTERRAIN*, among many other periodicals and anthologies. A native New Yorker, Nick now lives in California, but first he spent several years living in Jersey City, New Jersey.

EMB
RACE
THE
ODD

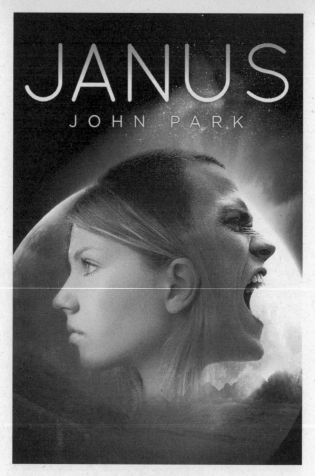

JANUS

JOHN PARK

AVAILABLE SEPTEMBER 2012

978-1-927469-10-1

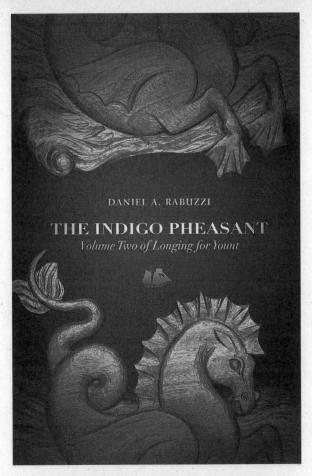

"Ian Rogers' stories are old-fashioned in the very best sense: classic chillers in the spirit of Shirley Jackson and Richard Matheson. *Every House Is Haunted* is full of well-crafted, satisfying twists, a fine companion for any reader of literate horror."
—Andrew Pyper, author of *Lost Girls*, *The Killing Circle*, and *The Guardians*

EVERY HOUSE IS HAUNTED
IAN ROGERS

AVAILABLE OCTOBER 2012

978-1-927469-16-3

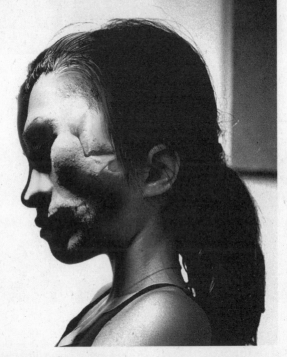